There was s
over her face

She was in a bli
something of the world around her but not
wanting to wake and cope with any problems.

Then the something moving over her face
kissed her, and she had to wake up. There was
Steve looking down at her.

She looked beyond him to the sky. The sun
had gone in and the sky was darker, hazier. If
anything it was warmer, and the stillness full
of foreboding.

Slowly, she sat upright, yawned. 'I enjoyed
that little sleep. Did you sleep too?'

'Perhaps a bit. But most of the time I just
looked at you.'

She didn't know what to say to this. Certainly
didn't want to talk about what they had just
done. It was too close, too wonderful…

NURSING SISTERS

**Nursing might be their first love—
but it won't be their last...**

Kate and Jo Wilde are dedicated to each other as sisters and dedicated to their nursing careers. They've both never been short of admirers, but Kate has never looked for love and finds it a problem when love finds her. While Jo, always the home bird, open to stability, love and marriage, finds herself jilted at the altar. Both have the strength of character to fight their way through their disappointments and dilemmas to find their own kind of happiness.

THE NURSE'S DILEMMA is Kate's story.

**Look out for Jo's story,
coming soon in Mills & Boon® Medical Romance™**

THE NURSE'S DILEMMA

BY
GILL SANDERSON

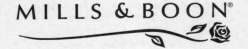

MILLS & BOON®

FOR PAULA AND IAN—WITH LOVE.

First published in Great Britain 2001
Harlequin Mills & Boon Limited,
Eton House, 18-24 Paradise Road, Richmond, Surrey TW9 1SR

© Gill Sanderson 2001

ISBN 0 263 82669 4

Set in Times Roman 10½ on 12 pt.
03-0601-50710

Printed and bound in Spain
by Litografia Rosés, S.A., Barcelona

CHAPTER ONE

THE cream Mercedes pulled up outside the departure hall of McCarran International airport, Las Vegas. Kate Wilde took a silver-paper-covered box from beside her and she and her American friend Lucy McTurk scrambled out of the back doors.

The driver walked round to fetch Kate's luggage. He dumped it disapprovingly at her feet. 'I'll park the car and then see you inside,' he said. 'Why don't you go inside where it's cool?'

The two girls watched him carefully drive away. Then, 'Is this really all that you're taking?' Lucy asked, looking amazed at Kate's battered blue rucksack. 'Have you got enough clothes here? I take double that just for a weekend.'

'There's enough here for a fortnight,' Kate said happily. 'You know I always travel light. That bag has got all I need, all the essentials. It's carried me through three continents over the past five years. Besides, there's a wonderful new dress waiting for me at home.'

At home. It seemed an odd phrase to use; she didn't really have a home. She shrugged, and dismissed the thought.

Then she lifted the front of her baggy white T-shirt to reveal a money belt tight round her neat waist. 'I've got my bag strapped here with everything really important in it.' Including the little blue-wrapped packet, she remembered. She was not letting that out of her sight.

Lucy surveyed her friend affectionately: a slim, dark-haired figure, clad in T-shirt and jeans, disreputable espadrilles, and with a tracksuit top hung over her shoulders. She didn't look like an inter-continental traveller. 'Let's get into the shade,' she said.

It was about ninety degrees, typical for noon at this time of year in Las Vegas. The sun burned down with a dry desert heat. Kate picked up her rucksack, and the two crossed to the automatically opening doors and the instant chill of the air-cooled terminal building. Kate felt the usual little shock that came with entering any building in Las Vegas: the movement from heat to cold.

'We've got time for a soda before you fly,' Lucy said. 'And we can have a quick girlish word now about John Bellis out there, before he comes back. What are you going to do about him, Kate? He's nuts about you.'

Kate sighed. 'I like him; we've dated a couple of times. He's going to be a good surgeon one day. He's helped me a lot with my application for training, and I'm grateful. But he'll never be more than a friend to me. I've tried to tell him that without hurting him, but he just doesn't seem to want to know.'

'That's the trouble with surgeons, they get too focused, can only hold one thought at a time. So there's no chance for John at all?'

'I wish he'd realise that,' Kate said glumly. 'But I do like him and I don't want to hurt him.'

Fortunately there was no queue at check-in. She handed in her ticket, went through the usual questions of 'Have you packed your bag yourself?' and so on, and checked in her rucksack and her silver package. Then she took her boarding card. There was an hour before the plane departed. She went to find John and Lucy in the lounge.

They were sitting by the window. John fetched her a

cola, and Kate looked across the busy airport. It was a view she never tired of.

She could see the end of Las Vegas Boulevard—'The Strip'. There was the pyramid and Sphinx of Luxor, the green glass of MGM, the multicolour of Camelot. Close behind them was the dark line of the mountains where she had hiked so often. She could just see the Red Rock Canyon Conservation area, with Turtlehead Peak just in view.

The friends she wrote to at home didn't really understand why she had stayed so long in Las Vegas. She was an outdoor girl; what was she doing in that neon city? They didn't understand that she stayed for the walking, not the gambling. The Grand Canyon, Death Valley, Lake Mead—all were within a couple of hours' drive. Las Vegas was the best centre she knew for walking.

'I still don't see why you have to fly to England right now,' John said abruptly. 'Important decisions are being made about your future. You should be here to argue your case.'

Kate sighed. 'John, I'm going to England for the wedding of my twin sister. She's the only relation I have in the world, the person I love the most—even if I don't see her all that often. Of course I've got to go to England. If it was your sister getting married, wouldn't you go to her wedding—no matter what it cost you?'

The moment she asked the question she realised it was the wrong one. For John, work was all-important. 'I'd go—just for the day,' he said.

'Well I'm going to be Jo's bridesmaid, and I want to get there well before the ceremony. And I'm really looking forward to it.'

'Every girl wants to be a bridesmaid at least once,' Lucy put in. Then she added mischievously, 'And that way you get to grab the bride's bouquet. It means you get married next.'

Kate gritted her teeth when she saw how pleased John looked at this idea.

'The real reason I'm sorry to be going is that my application for training's coming up,' she said. 'John, I'm grateful for what you're doing for me.'

Although Kate was only at the hospital as a temporary nurse she knew she had a good reputation in the Emergency Room—what, in Britain, would be called the Accident and Emergency Department. The hospital had offered her the chance to train on a new course it was running for International Emergency Response nurses. These would be part of a team that was ready to fly to any part of the world where there was a disaster—flood, earthquake, fire, volcano eruption. It sounded like the ideal job for her—it involved travel and nursing. But there were plenty of applications, and she might lose her chance of getting on the course if she wasn't around. Still...

'I think you'd be good for the job,' John said soberly. 'I'm sure the offer will still be open in a fortnight.'

Kate finished her cool drink. 'Time I went to the Departure lounge,' she said, 'Lucy, John, it was good of you to bring me.'

There was an affectionate hug from Lucy, and an embrace from John that he tried to make into something more than it was. Gently, she disengaged herself from him. Then she walked quickly to the lounge entrance, showed her boarding pass and was allowed inside. A quick wave to her two friends and she was on her own.

Kate sat down by the window again; there was a better view here. For three-quarters of an hour she could watch the planes come and go. McCarran was a busy airport, with planes landing practically every minute. She felt the excitement that always came when she was about to travel.

There was the crackle of a loudspeaker; her flight was being called. She bought a couple of bottles of water, then walked towards her gate. By now she knew how to tackle the long-haul flights.

Her flight would take about ten hours. It would set off in the afternoon, but, since it lost hours and wouldn't arrive in England until the following morning, it was in effect overnight. But she knew how to cope.

On board the plane there was a scuffle for locker space, the usual announcements, the smiles of the stewards. Then the long taxi to the beginning of the runway, the howl of the raced engines and the bumpy acceleration. Finally the easy leap into the air. She loved it!

Kate had a window seat and she peered at the badlands below, where she had walked, the lake where she had so often bathed. After an hour or so the first meal was served. Then it was time to put on her tracksuit top and pull the hood firmly over her face. She pushed in earplugs and went to sleep. For the rest of the flight she would eat nothing, and drink nothing but water. Alcohol might be fun, but the pressure difference made it stronger and she would pay the price when she landed. This way she would arrive reasonably fresh. Kate was going home.

Dr Steve Russell stood and shivered on the observation deck of Manchester airport. It might soon be the May Bank Holiday, but at this time in the morning it was chilly. However, sometimes he felt that too much of his time was spent in surgeries, wards and bedrooms, so he liked to get in the open air when he had the chance.

The plane holding the person he was to meet had landed, and was taxiing slowly across the tarmac. There was no need yet to go down; reclaiming baggage, Customs and Immigration would take another half-hour. He didn't want to mix with the throngs downstairs. For a while he was happy with his own company. It gave him a chance to think—even though some of his thoughts weren't exactly happy.

Being best man for his cousin Harry was harder work than he had realised. 'You brought us together; it's only right that you should see us married,' Harry had said cheerfully, taking things for granted, as he always did. At first Steve had thought that all he would have to do was pass over a ring and toast the bridesmaids. But there was so much to do! And Harry had seen that Steve did his share.

Now he had been asked to pick up Kate, Jo's twin sister. Jo had intended to do it, but an early-morning meeting with her dressmaker had made things difficult—so Steve had volunteered.

He'd never met Kate. He wasn't really sure he wanted to. Jo had said that he'd have no difficulty in recognising her; the two of them were almost identical. Jo was marrying his cousin and his friend Harry Russell. Steve had come to accept that, and to look as if he was happy about it—he had had to. But meeting a twin sister—who looked like Jo, apparently sounded like her, had a similar character—it was going to be hard. It was going to hurt.

He shivered again. A light rain had started to fall. Perhaps he would go downstairs; there was time for a quick coffee. The presence of other people might stop him thinking about himself.

It was supposed to be early summer in Manchester. But it was grey and raining, and compared to Las Vegas it was decidedly cool. Kate shivered, glad of her tracksuit top.

Jo had said she would meet her. But as the crowd spilled out into the reception area there was no sign of her sister. All around her people were being greeted, kissed, hugged. But there was no one for her.

'You're Kate Wilde; you just must be. Kate, you're as gorgeous as your sister.'

Well, that was quite a nice greeting, really. Kate looked at the man who had spoken to her, very ready to approve of him. It wasn't hard.

At first she'd thought it was Harry Russell, the man about to become her brother-in-law. Jo had sent her a couple of photographs of him. But then she realised that, although there was a resemblance, this wasn't him. Both men were tall, well-built, dark-haired. But this man, casually dressed in red checked shirt and cord trousers, didn't have Harry's rather excessive good looks.

He wasn't smiling either. If anything he looked rather solemn. His eyes were dark grey, and for a moment Kate thought she could read a touch of fugitive pain there. But then why should he be sad? She was imagining things.

'I'm Kate Wilde, and I rather like being called gorgeous. But who're you?'

The man leaned forward and slipped the rucksack from her shoulder. It was heavier than it looked but he handled it with ease. 'I'm Steve Russell. I'm going to be best man a week today. Jo sends her apologies, but she had an urgent meeting with her dressmaker and so I volunteered to pick you up. Getting married is far harder work than I had realised, Kate. The things you have to remember!'

'So you're not married yourself?' she asked boldly.

'Not married, no prospect of getting married, no great urge to get married either.' He smiled at her cheerfully. 'But I am looking forward to next Saturday's festivities.'

When he smiled his face changed. It became alive. It said that this man was your friend. She just had to smile back.

'Are all the wedding arrangements finished, then?'

'More or less, I think. Your sister is a brilliant or- ganiser. She ought to be a hospital administrator or something high-powered like that.'

'She always was that way. We might look alike, but we have totally different characters. She's the home- builder, the careful planner. I'm the careless one.'

'Totally different?' he mused. 'I wonder. Anyway, d'you want to stop here for anything or shall we go straight to see your sister?'

She looked round the busy concourse. 'This feels like coming home,' Kate said. 'Let's go. Just one thing. Everyone else is being kissed as a welcome back. I'm so happy to be here, so...' She leaned forward, took Steve's forearms in her hands and kissed him. It was just a quick kiss, the merest brush of her lips on his. It was meant to be friendly, brotherly, even. But she felt the swell of the muscles in his arms, and her breasts touched his chest.

'That's not much of a kiss,' he said. He dropped her rucksack, wrapped both arms round her and pulled her close. His lips found hers. He kissed her gently, as she had kissed him. But then his kiss became different; it was passionate, demanding. At first she was shocked— but then she thought she liked being held so tightly, kissed with such ardour. Suddenly he released her. His face was troubled. 'Perhaps I shouldn't have done that,' he said.

She didn't know how to reply to that. 'Perhaps you shouldn't,' she mumbled after a while. 'But I wasn't objecting. Shall we go now?'

Wordlessly, he picked up her rucksack and led her out of the terminal.

By unspoken joint consent they didn't refer to the brief flare of emotion both had felt when he'd kissed her. It had been a sudden, unexpected thing. They would both forget it.

They talked casually as he drove. He had a large blue estate car, the back seat littered with assorted medical pamphlets. He told her that he was a GP with a practice in the town, that he'd known Harry for years and Jo quite a while. He was interested when she told him that she worked in an Emergency Room in Las Vegas.

'I'm going to spend some time in the local hospital A and E Department,' he said. 'GPs can work on the wards, and hospital doctors have some time seeing what a GP's job is like. Both sides get to understand the other's problems. I'm down to spend a few sessions in A and E quite soon.'

'Sounds a good idea,' Kate said. Her eyes closed and she forced them open again. She had to stay awake for the rest of the day. 'I still feel you're driving on the wrong side of the road,' she said.

He laughed. 'You'll get used to it.' After that they said little.

* * *

They moved from the M62 to the M6 and then turned off left. It was an hour's drive to the little town of Kirkhelen, and they approached it across the Lancashire Plain. The town stood on a hill, and after a while Kate could see the church on the top of the hill, where Jo would get married.

As they approached Kate felt a bewildering set of emotions. They passed the site where she'd used to camp with the Girl Guides, the river where they'd used to paddle. The two of them had been brought up here; Jo had spent all her life here. But the moment Kate had qualified, she had gone away. She was a wanderer, she had no feelings for home. But now there was the vague feeling that she might be missing something. Would she go wandering again?

She was jet-lagged, she decided. Long-distance travel could affect your mind as well as your body. This mood would soon pass.

They were almost at the town now. In the distance Kate could see the greenfield site that held the Milner General Hospital. On the right was a small estate of newly built houses. Steve turned into it.

'We're early,' he said, glancing at his watch. 'Kate, been good to meet you. I'm sure we'll see a lot more of each other in the next few days.'

'You're not coming in?' she asked. She felt she'd like to see more of him—perhaps a lot more.

'Can't, I'm afraid. Harry and I are going walking in the Lakes for the rest of the day; he's been promising himself this last walk for a while now. Anyway, you'll have so much to say to your sister.'

'You're right. Steve, thanks for picking me up.'

He glanced at her. 'It was a pleasure,' he said. 'I enjoyed meeting you.'

She wondered if the casual, polite words carried a hidden meaning. Then she decided she was imagining things.

They pulled up outside a pretty detached house. It was obviously very new, but someone had been working in the front garden, putting in rows of bedding plants. The front door opened, and there was the figure she knew so well.

'Kate! You've come home.'

Kate jumped out of the car and ran to meet her sister.

Always, always, when she had been away, there was that strange feeling when she first saw her sister. That was her face, and her body—but somehow different. The clothes she didn't recognise. Then there was a feeling of wonder. Why did she spend so much time away from the person she knew best in all the world, the person who had been through so much with her? And this had been their longest period apart.

She ran over, hugged and kissed her sister. 'My older sister! Jo you look wonderful! Getting married must be good for you.'

'Oh, it is, Kate. You should try it.'

Kate held her sister at arm's length, looked at her critically. Jo was the older sister—by five minutes. And now there was a bloom about her, an aura of happiness. But to the trained eye there were signs of fatigue, slight bags under her eyes, and little lines by her mouth.

'Jo, you've been doing too much, haven't you? Not enough sleep?'

'Well, I'm still working, of course, and organising a wedding takes for ever! There have been times when we've wished we had eloped. But it's nearly all done now. Come on, let's go inside. Steve, thanks for picking up my sister.'

Kate was dimly aware that Steve was behind her, carrying her rucksack and the silver parcel. 'My pleasure,' he said. 'Hope to see you later, ladies.' And he was gone.

They left the rucksack in the hall and went into the newly furnished kitchen. With obvious pride Jo put on the kettle, took mugs from a cupboard. 'Tell me what you've been up to. I'm so happy I want to marry everybody off. You haven't got a man anywhere, I suppose?'

Kate shook her head. 'No man. Lots of male friends, but no special man. I'm beginning to doubt if I'll ever meet that one person I want to spend my life with. I've seen a bit of an American doctor, but... well, he's good-hearted but he's not for me. Nothing will come of it. Anyway, where's your man? What's Harry doing, going for a walk?'

'I've sent him away for the day. Both of us have been mad busy for the past four weeks—Katie, you don't know what hard work it is getting married. Anyway, he's been looking more and more harassed, so he's going off to the Lake District for a day's walking with Steve. Steve's nice, Kate, isn't he?'

'Very nice,' Kate agreed.

'I would have married Steve if I hadn't wanted to marry Harry. Oh, Kate, I know you're going to love Harry!'

'I'm sure I will.' Kate smiled. 'You know he rang me up in the middle of the night? He said he wanted to do the proper thing and ask a relative for your hand in marriage. And I was your only relative.'

'He's like that. He's impulsive.'

A part of Kate's mind carefully suppressed the thought that Harry could have worked out that eight a.m. in England was three o'clock in the morning in Las Vegas—and that she might not like being woken after the shift she had done. But that was nothing. Harry had sounded really excited, and she liked him for that. She knew he was a doctor in the Milner General Hospital, where Jo worked—a junior registrar in Orthopaedics.

'So how are the wedding plans going? Anything I can do to help at this late stage?'

'You know me, always organised. I've got this vast folder of plans and a countdown worked out. You've got to try your bridesmaid's dress; I think you'll like it.' Jo looked at her sister critically. 'The dress fits me perfectly, but I think perhaps you're a bit thinner. You can try it on in a few minutes and we can phone for the dressmaker to call in tomorrow if necessary.'

'So, am I the only bridesmaid?'

'No, two little girls as well. They're Andrew's daughters—you know, the consultant I work for.'

'Andrew Kirk. You've talked about him before.'

'I'm going to carry on working for him until Harry and I decide… Well, that's in the future. Anyway, you'll meet the little girls on Thursday evening. We're having a rehearsal in church. I want everything to .go as planned.'

Kate looked at her sister affectionately. The two were fraternal, not truly identical twins. And, although they looked so alike, they both knew they were vastly different in character. Jo had always been the planner: working out her holidays, buying her clothes according to a budget, deciding on which bit of nursing would provide her with an interesting career. Kate had been the madcap, always wanting to know what was over the horizon, never staying anywhere for long. Perhaps that was why they got on so well together.

'How long are you staying, Kate? The wedding's next week, then we're having a fortnight's honeymoon in Venice…it'd be lovely if you were around when we got back. You could get a job at my hospital! They're desperately short of nurses. Stay with us a while.'

'Stay with a newly married couple? Never! You don't want to start married life with a sister in the spare bedroom.' Kate shrugged uneasily. 'No, there's work in Vegas as long as I want it, and it's well paid too. And there's a chance of training for an emergency response team. I think I'll go back after the wedding.'

'Time you settled down,' Jo teased. 'Like I am.'

'You've *always* been settled down. I've never known anyone like you, who knew what she wanted and went out to get it. Now, tell me, is there anyone I know who will be coming to this wonderful affair…?'

Later, Jo took her sister on a tour of inspection. 'I know it's only small, but we wanted to buy our first house, and we can move up to a bigger one when we start a family.' Jo looked out at the garden proudly. 'We've been living here together for three months now—well, people do, don't they? But I've kicked him out for a fortnight before the wedding. He's staying with Steve. Come and look round and tell me what you think.'

In fact Kate liked it already. The house stood on the side of a hill and there was a view across the valley. Unusually for a modern house, there appeared to be a reasonable-sized garden. She liked the inside as well. It was still half furnished, of course—but it was comfortable. On the walls were enlarged pictures of herself and

Jo, taken through the years. She had copies of the same photographs in her wallet, and on her wall in Las Vegas. This was more than a house; it was already a home.

'D'you want a bath?' Jo asked when they had finished looking round. 'You can try on your bridesmaid's dress straight after.'

'Good idea. Flying long distance always makes me feel a bit grubby. But first—you can buy anything in Las Vegas.' She reached round the back of her T-shirt and unfastened the belt that held her ticket, her passport and her money. It also held the small blue-paper-wrapped packet. She opened it.

'You said that Harry wore a gold chain, so I guessed he wouldn't mind male jewellery. This is a pair of amethyst and silver cufflinks. They're a traditional Navaho pattern.'

'Kate, they're lovely!' Jo peered into the little box. 'When we get married he says he's going to wear cufflinks from his cricket club. Well, he's just changed his mind.'

'Let him decide that,' Kate advised. 'The love of a man for his cricket club is not to be trifled with. Anyway, this is for you.'

In silence Jo accepted the package Kate was offering her. It was a choker, in solid silver, with a red symbol engraved on it. 'Navaho art again,' Kate said. 'That symbol means long life and happiness.'

'Long life and happiness. It's what I'm going to have. I'll wear this, Kate. It'll go so well with the neckline of my dress. Oh, it's so good to have you back! I wish you'd stay.'

'We'll have to see,' Kate said gently. 'Now, what was that about a bath?'

She was shown into a bedroom, only half furnished.

But in the built-in cupboard there was a long lilac dress, covered in a Polythene envelope. 'Your bridesmaid's dress,' Jo said proudly. 'I know you'll look good in it. I'm in white, of course. But the dressmaker said this suited my colouring, so it should suit yours. By the way, I've booked an appointment for you at the hairdresser's at the same time as me. Is that all right?'

'Jo! You've planned everything!'

'You know me, I like to get things right. But have a bath now, and then we'll have a trying-on session.'

Kate felt better after the bath. She put on clean underwear and then tried on the bridesmaid's dress. Jo smoothed it on her, adjusting the shoulders, then turned Kate to the full-length mirror. 'What do you think?'

Well, her hair needed attention, she definitely needed make-up, and she needed a pair of heels—but otherwise... 'I look gorgeous,' she said modestly.

'You do.' But Jo's voice was critical. All was not yet completely perfect. 'But I think...just a tiny touch too loose here,' she muttered, pulling at the waist. 'It'll only take the dressmaker a minute to put that right.'

Kate smiled to herself. She loved this almost obsessive trait in her sister. 'What about flowers?' she asked.

'I'm having roses—red roses. I know they're a bit conventional, but who cares? I'm a conventional girl. Now, come into my bedroom and we'll see how we look together.'

It was a simple white raw-silk wedding dress, with a white cap and a veil. Jo had been right; the Navaho choker Kate had bought her matched it perfectly. The two sisters stood side by side, looking into the mirror.

'Now we're both gorgeous,' Kate said with satisfaction. She said the words light-heartedly, as a little joke. Right now she didn't want to be serious. But she knew

what she'd said was true. They were striking, a lovely
pair. Impulsively, she leaned over to kiss her sister. 'Nobody who sees you will ever forget you,' she said.

'Nobody who sees us will ever forget us,' Jo corrected. 'Don't forget, you're my bridesmaid only on
condition that I can be your matron of honour.'

'It's a deal. But don't hold your breath.'

Jo picked up the skirt of her dress, pirouetted round
the room. 'I feel so happy in this,' she said, 'so I'm
going to take it off and you can wear it for a minute.
Perhaps it'll have some weird effect and you'll want to
get married yourself.'

'I need to find a man first, and at the moment there
aren't many around who are suitable. But I do want to
try it on.'

When Kate did try on the dress it had an odd effect
on her. This was a wedding dress, suitable for nothing
but getting married in. She thought she looked well in
it. But there was something else—almost a feeling of
anticipation. It might be fun to get married.

'You like yourself in it, don't you?' Jo asked. The
two could always read each other's moods.

'I must be more jet-lagged than I realised,' Kate replied. 'Marriage isn't for me—not yet.' She irritably
reached for the zip.

There was one more thing to be tried on. Kate ran
downstairs and fetched the silver-wrapped box she had
packed so carefully. 'Have you decided on a going-
away dress yet?' she asked.

Jo frowned. 'I've got a couple that will do, but I
haven't made up my mind yet. Why?'

Kate pushed the box towards her. 'This is a little
extra going-away present.'

Jo pulled at the silver paper, tore away the bubble

wrap. And there, wrapped finally in tissue paper, was a blue silk trouser suit. She lifted it, pressed it to her face. 'Kate, this is beautiful.'

'It'll fit you,' said Kate. 'It fits me.'

By now Kate was feeling tired, but she knew the best thing to do was not to sleep until night. She had to force her body into a new time pattern, she had done it before. Besides, she was a nurse, accustomed to disturbed sleep patterns. Working in A and E, she had discovered that people would injure themselves at the oddest times of day and night.

Together they went through the folder of wedding plans. The organisation was fantastic! There were copies of business letters sent, invitations sent and acceptances noted, presents received. There was a timetable, a seating plan, a note of those guests who were vegetarian. On each day for the past fortnight there had been a set of tasks to do, and each task had been neatly ticked off.

'You should have had this on computer,' Kate said, only half joking, 'on a spreadsheet. Or I'm sure there's software for planning a wedding.'

Jo looked thoughtful. 'There probably is,' she said. 'I wish I had thought of that. There wouldn't have been all this crossing out and writing in again.'

Kate managed not to let her sister see her smile. What a manager had been lost when Jo had become a theatre nurse!

The rain had stopped but it was still not very warm. Jo lent her a thin coat and they walked up through town to the church. 'We'll have a proper rehearsal on Thursday evening,' Jo said, 'but I want you to get the feel of the place. The flowers will be here early on Saturday morning.'

Kate glanced round the dim interior, looked at the stained glass, the vaulting roof. The church was over three hundred years old. It would please her to get married here herself—not that she was intending to get married!

On their way down the hill they called in at the White Hart, the hotel where the reception would take place. There was another wedding dinner being held there. Jo was obviously well known at the place by now, and the two of them were invited to peer in at the function room and see how well it looked. At one end of the room was a small table with a three-tiered cake. Jo smiled. 'Did I show you the picture of my cake?' she asked.

When they were together the two sisters always shared their emotions. If one was happy, the other had to be. By now Kate was feeling the excitement, the anticipation, even the apprehension that Jo was feeling. The week coming was going to be exhausting! But she was looking forward to every minute of it. And she could help.

It was now Sunday afternoon, she had left Las Vegas on Saturday afternoon. And although it was only twenty-four hours ago, it now seemed like ages.

'Are you still working in Theatre?' she asked.

'Until Thursday night. Andrew, my boss, wanted me to take off longer, but he has a big list on Thursday and I know he likes working with me. You'll like the staff; they're all coming to the wedding. Like I said, Andrew's two daughters are going to be your sister-bridesmaids, they're sweet little girls. And we've just got a new man as senior registrar, called Ben Franklin, I've only met him once but I've invited him because I want the whole team there. And after the wedding—the

honeymoon...a fortnight in Venice! Kate, I can't believe it's finally going to happen!'

'You've no idea how it makes me happy to see you
happy,' Kate said, 'and I think Harry is a very lucky
man indeed. Anyway, why shouldn't it happen?'

For the first time she saw her sister slightly in doubt.
'Well, Harry's a bit of an oddball in some ways. He has
these sudden enthusiasms and then...' She shrugged. 'I
guess I'm just getting a bit strained.'

'I'm sure you are,' Kate said, 'and you're entitled to
be.' She stood and stretched. 'I suppose I ought to un-
pack.'

'That blue rucksack. Harry asked me what he should
get you as a bridesmaid's present. I was tempted to say
a new rucksack.'

'It's part of me now.' Kate yawned. 'I'll never get
rid of it. Be down in five minutes.'

It was now nearly tea-time, and Jo went to the kitchen
as Kate unpacked her few things and hung them or put
them in the empty drawers. She had treated herself to
a set of silk underwear for the wedding, but otherwise
her clothes were those that she'd proved over the years.

She heard a car draw up outside. For a while the
engine continued running, even though it was obvious
that the car was not moving. Casually, she walked to
the window, peered round the edge of the curtain. It
was Steve's blue car. Kate felt a moment's pleasure.
She'd like to see Steve again. The car engine stopped.

But Steve didn't get out. She could see him, just sitting, dressed in the same red checked shirt. He was just
staring out of the window. There was no one else in the
car, no sign of the Harry she had been expecting to
meet. It seemed a little—odd.

Then the driver's door slowly opened and Steve did

get out. She leaned back behind the curtain, not wanting to be thought a nosy neighbour or anything.

He shut the car door and stood by it, looking at the house as if searching for something. She shrank further behind the curtain; he couldn't see her. He seemed hesitant, as if not wanting to come in. Then he appeared to make up his mind. His shoulders were braced; she could almost see the determination there.

She felt the first tingle of apprehension. There was something wrong. Where was Harry? Why was he back so early? Why was this man putting off coming to the house?

She watched him stride down the path, heard the muted ring of the doorbell. She heard Jo open the door.

Her bedroom door was open; she could clearly hear what was said in the hall below. Jo's voice, bright, bubbling, happy as she'd been all day. 'Hi, Steve, back early, aren't you? Where's Harry?'

There was the mutter of a male voice, Kate couldn't hear what was said. Then the sound of the living room door shutting.

There was something oppressive about the silence. Kate caught herself listening, straining to hear what came next.

Then it came, a scream of anguish that she could barely recognise as coming from her sister. 'No! He can't! Steve, this is some kind of joke, you can't mean it! Steve? *Steve!*'

Kate rushed downstairs, threw open the door of the new, barely furnished living room. Steve was standing by the fireplace, an anguished expression on his face. He was trying to fend off Jo, who was ineffectually hitting his chest and arms, sobbing at the same time. Jo was more upset than Kate had ever seen. There was a piece of paper in Jo's hand. It fluttered to the floor as Kate pulled her sister round, held her, hugged her. Jo wept on her shoulder.

Kate just didn't know what to do. She glanced at Steve, who just stood, a picture of misery. 'Jo, what's the matter? Jo, it's me, it's Kate. Come on, tell me. What's the matter? Has anyone hurt you?'

Under her arms, she could feel the frantic thudding of her sister's heart, feel her chest heaving with weeping. Then Jo broke away, picked up the piece of paper from the floor, stared at it as if she couldn't believe in it. Then she thrust it at Kate.

'It's a letter—a letter from Harry. He says he doesn't want to marry me, can't marry me. He's gone abroad.'

CHAPTER TWO

KATE read the letter over Jo's shoulder. It was short, stark. *Thinking of getting married had been a mistake. Better to find out now. Still love you.*

Her arms were round her sister, holding her to her. Never had she seen Jo so upset. She could feel her body racked by sobs and she wondered if the crying would ever stop. They were orphans, they had been through hard times together, but never had there been suffering like this. This was the worst.

She wondered exactly what had happened. How could Jo have fallen for a man who turned out to be so cruel, so cowardly? Her anger was rising, but she knew better than to let it blaze through. It wouldn't help Jo, and now all she had to concentrate on was comforting her sister.

'You've got me, Jo,' she crooned. 'You've got me. We're sisters, we'll hang together.' She rocked her the way they'd used to hold and rock each other when they were children, when one was in pain or in trouble. Perhaps Jo's sobbing grew less.

Kate looked up at Steve angrily. 'You can go now,' she said. 'I think you've done enough for one day, haven't you?'

But even in her own distress she could see that he was upset too. Like a man, he tried to hide it, to remain imperturbable, but Kate could see the signs of strain in his face.

She was rather surprised when he did walk out of the

room, but instead of walking through the front door he went to the kitchen. Two minutes later he returned with a cup of tea in his hand. 'Try this,' he said gently to Jo. 'It might make you feel a little better.'

With a rare burst of temper Jo slapped the cup out of his hand. It smashed against the wall, and tea dripped down over the fresh paint. 'I don't want tea! I want nothing from you! Why didn't you try to stop him? You're supposed to be his friend as well as his cousin. And I thought you were my friend too!'

'It's been as big a shock to me as to you, Jo. I'm so sorry.' He stooped to pick up the pieces of the broken cup. Then he walked back to the kitchen and returned with another cup of tea. This time he held it, and looked enquiringly at Kate. 'I do think you ought to try to drink some, Jo,' he said.

Kate took the cup and held it to her sister as if she were a baby. 'Come on, big sister,' she said gently. 'See if you can drink this. It'll stop you crying.'

This time Jo didn't knock the cup away. She drank the tea, and her sobbing subsided a little. Then she moved over to the couch and sat, knees tight together, face hidden in her hands. Steve looked at the still figure broodingly, then left the room again.

When he returned he held a glass of water and a pill. 'I think you should take this,' he said to Jo.

'What is it?' Kate asked suspiciously.

'It's a sedative. I'm Jo's GP. She needs rest now, probably sleep. Can we get her upstairs?'

'I'll take her,' said Kate. 'I think she's had enough help from men for a while.' She reached for the water and pill and offered them to Jo, who dutifully took both. Kate thought a moment and then said, 'And forget what

I said earlier about leaving. You'd better stay here; there are things I need to know.'

He didn't reply.

Somehow, Kate managed to get her sister upstairs. She helped her undress, then sat by her till the tear-swollen eyes closed. She didn't know what the sedative was, but it was certainly effective. Just as she was tip-toeing out of the bedroom she saw, of all things, a man's set of pyjamas, neatly folded. She took them down to the kitchen and stuffed them into the bin. Feeling just a tiny bit better, she went back to the living room.

Steve was still standing by the fireplace. 'She's asleep,' said Kate. 'What did you give her?'

'Diazepam. I wouldn't normally use it, I think it can get too addictive, but this time circumstances made it necessary. She'll probably wake up in a couple of hours, though.' His voice was flat, emotionless.

'Right,' said Kate, and went to sit on the couch. 'So now you and me can have a little talk. There are a lot of questions that need answering.'

He looked at her. 'You want to ask about Harry and what part I played in everything. Fine. But you're not in a fit state to ask questions, and I don't much feel like answering them. Later on I will talk about him, but not now.'

Kate looked at him in amazement. 'You can stand there and say that?'

'I can because we've got other, more important things to do. We've got to cancel this wedding, write no end of letters, spare Jo as much pain as possible.'

'*We* don't have to do it. I have to do it,' snarled Kate. 'I don't need your help.'

'I appreciate your concern. But you do need my help.

I know most of what has gone on, and I know most of the people involved. I can make it easier for your sister than you can. Kate, I can't insist, but I want to help.'

She looked at him in silence for a minute. Then she sighed. What he said made sense.

Apparently he guessed what she was thinking. He said, 'Let me fetch you some tea, now, you look as if you need it. And I certainly want some myself. Or are you now a native American? Do you want coffee?'

'Tea, please,' she said. His words made her think of the cup Jo had smashed, and she looked at the wall. The traces of china had been swept up, and there was a damp patch where the wall had been sponged. She looked at Steve curiously. He had noticed her glance.

'I cleared up as best I could,' he said. 'In some ways I'm quite domesticated.'

While he was gone the anger boiled up in her again. She thought of her sister—what would she be feeling when she woke later? What had she done to deserve this? What kind of man was Harry to do this to her? What kind of man was Steve, to be Harry's best friend? He must have known something!

He returned with a tray holding two mugs of tea and a plate of biscuits. 'You know your way around here,' she said nastily.

'I've spent a lot of time here recently. May I suggest you eat a couple of biscuits? You're stressed and your blood sugar will be low.'

'Are you an expert on low blood sugar and stress?'

'I am a doctor, as I said, and I know you're stressed. I'm stressed myself. I know that you're really angry and that you've got cause to be. You want to hit out at someone, and I'm the obvious target. I don't mind; I sympathise. But you ought to know that I'm equally angry with him.'

She thought for a while and then said, 'No, not equally angry. Jo is my twin sister. Everything she feels, I feel. Anyway, what's this louse Harry to you?'

'He's nothing now.' He put the tray on the coffee table in front of her, pushed a mug towards her. For a moment she felt a touch ashamed of herself. It really didn't seem to be his fault. But she was so angry!

'Why don't you sit down?' she mumbled. 'If we've got to talk we might as well do it in comfort.'

Steve sat opposite her, still saying nothing. She drank her tea and did as he suggested, ate a couple of biscuits. Yes, she did feel a little better.

She had quite taken to Steve when he had met her this morning. He'd seemed pleasant, and the effect of that kiss had been—well, a shock. But then he had turned into a bringer of bad news, a target for her anger. Now she tried to look at him as a person again, someone who she would have to see a lot of. Already she'd noticed his dusty cords and checked shirt. He must have come straight to see Jo, resisting the temptation to go home first, to wash and change, anything to put off the awful job he had been given. Kate was now coming to realise that he really might feel as badly as she did.

'Look, I'm sorry for the way I acted,' she said. 'I know it's not your fault, and there's a little bit of me that recognises that you're suffering too. I want you to know that I appreciate what you're doing.'

'I'd do anything for Jo,' he said, 'and so by extension I'd do anything for you.' He smiled—a strained smile, but a smile all the same. 'This isn't the time to mention it, but when I met you this morning I thought that I'd very much enjoy walking down the aisle as best man with you at my side as chief bridesmaid.'

The smile disappeared, and suddenly he was businesslike. 'What d'you need to know?' he asked.

For one fleeting moment she thought that she too would have enjoyed walking down the aisle as bridesmaid with him as best man. But then she swept the thought aside. 'I know you said you didn't want to talk,' she said, 'but I do need to know a little bit about what happened. You can tell me. I'm quite calm now. And I know Jo will want to go over this time and time again. I need to be prepared.'

He took time to think about what she had said. Then, 'Jo might feel guilty herself when she's got over the initial shock. When the anger has gone it's quite common for there to be feelings of lack of worth. She'll wonder what she did wrong.'

'Are you a psychiatrist as well as a GP?' Kate snapped.

He shrugged. 'Any GP who doesn't look after the mind as well as the body is not much use,' he said. 'But I guess I'm not as good as I thought. I never expected this. Certainly he's been a bit pensive the last few days—but it seemed like pre-wedding nerves to me. I was completely wrong.'

She liked him for the stark honesty of his admission. She'd be honest herself. 'I'm sorry, I'm taking this out on you again,' she said, 'and I suspect that it won't be the last time.'

Again he smiled—and, just as she had noticed that morning, his face was transformed.

'I'll remember you said that. All right, I'll tell you what happened. Talking about it might help me understand it myself.'

He frowned, closed his eyes a minute. Then he opened them, looked straight at her. She knew that they were grey—but now she noticed they were flecked with little touches of green. Mysterious eyes. She wondered again if she had seen sadness in them that morning.

'I've known Harry Russell all my life,' he said. 'He's always been a bit of a chancer. When he was climbing, he'd always try a route a bit beyond his capacity. He gave up a couple of good jobs, hoping for something better. The surprising thing is that Harry's chancing usually worked out. He did well.'

'Tell me about him and Jo,' Kate said.

'Well, no girl was good enough for him for long. He had a long succession of very attractive girlfriends, but none of them lasted.'

'I'm beginning to think Jo is well rid of him,' Kate muttered.

'Possibly. You must understand he was—is—a charming man. Everyone liked him. He was always the centre of attention; he'd make you feel good. Anyway, about two years ago he started seeing your sister. I thought it wouldn't last, but it did. I liked Jo an awful lot—I still do—and I thought she'd be good for him. He settled down at last. I was really looking forward to being his best man.' He smiled again, but this time ruefully. 'I was looking forward to the wedding, to being best man, to meeting you, Kate.

'Then, over the past couple of weeks, after being really excited by all the preparations, Harry seemed a bit—well, thoughtful. Like I said, I thought it was nerves. Late last night he asked me to go to the Lake District for the day, a walk round the Kentmere fells. We didn't go in one car; he said he'd drive up and see me there. When we'd finished the walk, he gave me that letter and told me what he was doing. He didn't mention it once on the walk—we could at least have talked about it.'

Kate realised that thinking about what had happened was causing him genuine pain. But there was still more she needed to know herself. 'Did he give any reason?'

'No good one. What upset me was the realisation that he'd been planning this without saying anything. He's got all his stuff in order, agreed to take this job in Australia. I argued with him for an hour—till I felt like hitting him. I thought the very least he could do was tell Jo in person—but he wouldn't. Said he couldn't. I told him that if he got on that plane never to get in touch with me again. Our friendship was ended. But he still went.'

'Did you mean that about friendship? I thought men looked after each other.'

'Not always. Yes, I meant it. I know what it's like being ditched. I've been there...' Then he stopped.

'We'll have to go over all of this later,' he said. 'I'll be happy—' he corrected himself '—I'm willing to talk to Jo as long as she likes. But I do think you should be there as well. Now.' His voice altered, became flatter, more businesslike. 'We've got a wedding to cancel. Really, I suppose we should consult Jo.'

'Let's do all the preliminary work,' said Kate. 'Decide just who to write to, who I need to talk to in person. Then there's the church, the reception, the cars to cancel. I'll see if I can cancel the honeymoon; I don't think she'll want to go on her own.'

She went to the desk, took out the thick wedding folder and looked at it sadly. How different her feelings were from the last time she had looked at it! 'Jo was very efficient with her arrangements,' Kate said. 'It's going to make it easier to cancel. But there's a lot of work.'

'I've got a good practice manager called Vanessa Welsh. She could use the practice computer to do some of the work. It might simplify things, if you didn't mind.'

At first Kate thought she did mind, but then she saw the thickness of the folder. There was an awful lot of work. 'Will she be discreet?' she asked. 'And won't she mind the extra work?'

'I'll pay her for the extra work—and she works for doctors—she knows how to be discreet.'

'It sounds good, then,' Kate said. She looked at her watch—it was only seven in the evening! So much had happened and there was so much left to do. Her fatigue had left her, she had gone beyond it. She looked at Steve. She'd only met him a few hours ago, and yet she felt as if she'd known him for ever. She wasn't exactly calmer—but she knew now that she could cope.

Steve smiled at her again. 'We'll do what we can for Jo,' he said.

'It's good of you to offer to do so much. You must be busy in your own work.' Looking at him more closely, she realised there were lines of fatigue under his eyes, round his mouth. 'How long since you ate?' she asked abruptly. 'Apart from the biscuits, that is.'

He looked surprised. 'Breakfast, I guess,' he said, 'and a bar of chocolate on the walk. How did you know I was hungry?'

'Women's intuition. I'll do you a quick sandwich and then we'll start work. I'm hungry myself.'

Kate foraged in the kitchen, quickly made cheese and ham sandwiches and then put on a percolator of coffee. They were going to need all the caffeine they could get.

When she returned to the living room Steve was already making notes on a pad of scrap paper. 'First thing,' he said. 'Jo is a theatre nurse, and you know it's a job that requires total concentration. She was going to work the next four days, but I think I'll phone her consultant, explain what's happened and suggest she takes some time off. Andrew Kirk is a good friend; I know he'll understand. And he'll be able to get someone on his list for tomorrow.'

'That's a good idea,' she said cautiously. 'D'you want to phone before you eat?'

He did. They had a picnic meal together and afterwards she felt—well, less bad. Then she reached for the folder. Time to start work.

It was one o'clock in the morning when Steve let himself into his spartan little flat. He showered, and then poured himself a generous glass of malt whisky. He knew that problems were never solved by alcohol, but on this occasion he needed something to calm his whirling thoughts. Tomorrow he would be a busy doctor. His patients were entitled to his full attention.

The morning had started so well, and then it had turned into the worst day of his life. The sight of Jo's suffering had been almost more than he could bear. What was wrong with Harry? He must be mad! To give up someone like Jo...

And then there was Kate. When he had met her this morning he had been quite shocked. In fact he'd recognised her at once, but had waited quite a while before going over to speak to her. He'd had to get his thoughts in order. Someone who looked so like Jo—and yet was not her. She said they were different in character. Was that true? They still had an awful lot in common.

He closed his eyes, and images of the two flashed through his brain.

'You've been here all week now, Kate, and I don't know what I would have done without you. It's been terrible, but you and Steve have done everything for me. And you came here hoping to have a good time.'

'Happy to help in whatever way I can,' Kate said gently. 'Let's face it, that's what sisters are for. You know you'd do the same for me.'

This should have been the morning of the wedding, the happiest day of her sister's life. Kate snarled to herself, but said nothing.

'I suppose you'll have to go back soon,' Jo went on. 'But you will stay for the rest of the fortnight?' There was a wealth of sadness in her voice.

Kate had been thinking about this. She had come for the wedding, and then perhaps to spend a few days looking round, seeking memories of her youth. She hadn't been able to do it so far. But she didn't need to go back.

'I thought I might stay for a couple or three more weeks,' she said. 'Lodge with you if you'll have me. I've got quite a bit of money saved, and I'm quite enjoying it here.'

'You're going to stay! Kate, that'd be wonderful!'

When Kate heard the delight in her sister's voice, she knew that she couldn't go back straight away. This wasn't what she had intended—but it was what she was going to do.

There was a knock and then a shout through the open front door. 'Anyone home? It's Steve.'

'Come in, Steve,' Kate called. 'You always arrive just when we're going to have some tea.'

He appeared in the living room, dressed in dark blue jeans and T-shirt. As ever he looked well, his easy-moving body suited to the casual outfit. Kate was very pleased to see him—but she noticed the flash of pain across Jo's face. Jo liked Steve, was grateful for what he had done for her. But she had told Kate that he looked so like Harry. Every time Steve appeared, for a second Jo was reminded of her ex-fiancé. Kate could appreciate how much this hurt. She also suspected that Steve knew it too.

'Hi, Steve,' Jo said, falsely bright. Then, perhaps hearing something, she glanced out of the window that looked onto the back lawn. 'Oh, look! There's a kitten. Remember they called from across the road, saying they'd lost one? That must be it. Get Steve some tea, Kate, and I'll try to get hold of it.' Before either Kate or Steve could speak she had dashed out of the living room.

Steve looked at Kate questioningly. Kate nodded. They were both thinking the same thing. Although she was always polite to him, Jo seemed not to want to speak to Steve. 'It's all right,' he said, 'I understand. Because I remind her of Harry, part of her doesn't want to see me. Perhaps I shouldn't call as often.'

'No,' said Kate instantly, 'I think you should come as often as you can. Really, she likes you coming, you're supportive. And if you hadn't called over the past few days—well, my job would have been a lot harder.' Then she added, 'And I like seeing you too.'

Somehow, Steve had managed to call every day, partly as a GP, but mostly as a friend. Kate looked forward to his coming; it made a welcome break in the day.

'She won't come to me so I'm going to put her out

some milk and wait,' Jo called from the garden. 'You two drink your tea; I'll be in in a minute.' They heard her voice, 'Come on, puss, drink your nice milk…'

Steve closed the door and then sat on the couch next to Kate. 'How is she?' he asked.

Kate shrugged. 'Not as weepy as she was. Today's the day she should have got married, so I suggested that the pair of us go out for the day. She just wasn't interested. In fact she's not interested in anything. I've never seen her like this before.'

'This lassitude is a way of dealing with pain,' he told her. 'It'll pass in time. Then she might start passing through the angry stage. I don't think she should go back to work yet.'

'True. Andrew Kirk's been round quite often, though I've missed him. He's told her to take as long as she likes.'

'Good. You're in no hurry to get back to America? Nothing pulling you back?'

'I'll stay here as long as my sister needs me. There might be a time when leaving her would be the…proper thing to do. But it's not just yet. There's some training I might get but…I'll take my chance.' She wondered why he wanted to know.

'I've got her.' The door was pushed open, and there was Jo with a decidedly scruffy kitten in her arms. She was smiling. 'I'll just take her across the road; they'll be pleased to see her. Back in a minute, Steve.'

Through the large front window Kate could see her sister walking down the path. Jo had the kitten in her arms, was stroking it, talking to it. There was a lot of love there, Kate thought angrily, why did it have to go to waste?

Steve slid up the couch so he was by her side and,

like her, he looked out of the window. She could feel the touch of his shoulder on her arm, his hip next to hers. She had never got to like a man so quickly, she decided. Of course, there were reasons for this—circumstances had thrown them together. But now she could see Steve as a man, not just as her sister's GP. And he was quite definitely one of her friends.

'It's the first time all week she's shown any interest in anything or anyone,' Kate said. 'Perhaps it's a good sign.'

'It's certainly a good sign. Healing after this kind of trauma can be long and bitter.'

He seemed to speak with more intensity than usual, as if he could feel Jo's pain himself.

Kate had never been one to hang back. 'Are you speaking through personal experience?' she asked.

But he would not be drawn. 'A GP sees all kinds of grief,' he told her.

Together they watched Jo, her head bent over the cat, walk to the edge of the road. Casually, she glanced to the right. Then Kate saw the kitten jump out of her sister's arms; not thinking, Jo leaped forward after it. At that moment a car drove round the corner.

It wasn't travelling fast—but it was fast enough. The driver jerked at the wheel, the car swerved, Kate could hear the screech of tyres on the road.

Jo looked up, apparently paralysed. Kate heard herself scream—'Jo!'

There was a thump, and Jo was tossed in the air, arms windmilling. She hit the ground, rolled as the car came to a stop.

Kate saw the kitten trot across the road and scratch at the door where it lived.

Horrified, Kate turned to run to the door. Steve

grabbed her by the arm. 'Dial 999 and ask for an ambulance,' he snapped.

She paused. She had to get to her sister—but what he said made sense. Forcing herself to be calm, she dialled, passed on the message, and then ran outside herself.

There was a little group of neighbours round the prostrate body. The car driver, an elderly man, sat looking dazed. She knelt by her sister, opposite Steve, who was carefully feeling Jo's skull. Jo's face was too white, and there was a trickle of blood from a cut on her temple. This was her sister! But then her training snapped into place. She forced personal feelings to one side. She was an A and E nurse, accustomed to road traffic accidents.

The first thing always was to check ABC—airway, breathing, circulation. Steve nodded at her, he had already done it. 'Jo?' he was saying. 'Jo, can you hear me? Look at me.'

Slowly Jo's eyes opened. Steve bent over her, made sure the pupils were the same size—good, apparently no concussion. A neighbour ran back with Steve's bag from the back of his car. Steve flicked it open, took out a hard collar. 'I doubt this is necessary,' he muttered to Kate, 'but we'll make sure. Hold her head still, will you?'

As Kate steadied Jo's head he slipped the collar round her neck, fastened it tight. This was only a precaution in case of spinal injury. In A and E her neck would be X-rayed as a matter of course.

'Look at her leg,' Steve said. 'If we're in luck that will be the only major injury. But that's bad enough.'

Kate looked at the leg. It was distorted, at a highly

unnatural angle. An edge of white bone stuck through the skin. A compound fracture, and a bad one.

Jo should have been married today. This was going to be a doubly memorable day. In the distance Kate heard the siren of an ambulance.

CHAPTER THREE

BOTH Steve and Kate stood back to let the trained paramedics carefully lift Jo onto the stretcher and then into the ambulance. Then Kate travelled with her, leaving Steve to lock up and follow in his car. Once at the hospital Jo was treated as a priority case. Kate was told firmly but kindly that she must wait outside. Would she like anything and could she help fill in a few details? Then she could sit with her sister for a while.

Jo had been brought to the Milner Hospital, the one where she worked. Kate would have shamelessly said so, but it wasn't necessary. One of the senior nurses had trained and worked with her sister.

A couple of minutes later Steve walked in, sat by her and put his arm round her shoulders. It was comforting. 'There's a team looking at her now,' Kate said in a monotone. They say her leg has a bad fracture—but there doesn't appear to be anything life-threateningly wrong with her.'

'Waiting is the hard part,' Steve said. 'But there'll be someone to see us in a minute. This place has a good reputation.' In fact, when she could think as a professional, Kate was impressed by the department. It was well-run and efficient.

And only five minutes later a tall young doctor came in to see them and greeted Steve as an old friend. 'Steve! Good to see you! You're not...?'

'I'm not here professionally; I'm a friend of the family. This is Kate Wilde, sister of the injured girl.'

The doctor shook hands with her. 'My name's Nathan Brand. I'm junior registrar here.' He looked at Kate with a smile. 'I don't need telling—I can see that you're the patient's sister. Well, there doesn't seem to be anything wrong with Jo apart from the broken leg—but that's bad enough. She's got a compound fracture of the tib and fib, and it's far beyond my powers to set so I've sent for our Orthopaedic Consultant; he'll be here in an hour or so. Then I'm afraid it will be quite a long operation and a lengthy stay in hospital after that. I gather she's Andrew Kirk's theatre nurse?'

Kate nodded. 'And a friend of his.'

'Well, I don't fancy telling him that she's broken her leg; he'll go spare without her. I gather she's quite exceptional at her job.'

Hesitantly, Kate said, 'Recently my sister suffered…some emotional trauma. Will that affect her recovery, d'you think?'

The doctor looked grave. 'Well, it certainly won't help. But if she has support, if she has friends and relations round her, then she should be all right. Or we can always arrange counselling. Now, she's half asleep at the moment, but I know you'll want to go and see her. Is there anything else I can help you with?'

'Well,' said Kate, 'I'm a trained nurse, if you're looking for help at all?'

The doctor looked at her, not knowing what to make of this.

'You go to see Jo,' said Steve. 'I'll wait for you in the hospital canteen.'

In fact there was only time for a two-minute visit to a barely conscious Jo before the consultant came bustling in. He had hurried, as he wanted to get started. He was a short, bald little man, with a ferocious-looking white moustache and the broad, muscular hands of a pianist.

'A and E nurse, are you?' he barked. 'Well, look here.' He pointed to the X-rays lined up on a light source. 'We're going to have to clear out all these chips of bone, get this realigned and put in a pin here and here. Going to take quite some time. She'll limp for a while, but if she keeps up with the physiotherapy she should be all right. If I don't get her back in his theatre Andrew will never forgive me. Come down and see how we're doing in a couple of hours.'

'All right,' said Kate. For the first time she felt that things might not be all bad.

'Did you mean it about getting a job here or were you passing the time of day?' Steve asked.

They were sitting together in the hospital canteen, playing with drinks that neither of them wanted.

'I meant it,' she said. 'Don't forget, I am a qualified nurse. Like you, I trained in Liverpool. And wherever I've worked I've tried to get local accreditation. I could fit into that A and E Department straight away.'

'But I thought your intention was to go back to America.'

'It was. First I was coming for a fortnight, just for the wedding. But I decided early this morning that I'd stay an extra week or two—until I thought Jo was ready to start her life again. And now this accident. It's a nasty combination, a badly broken leg and an emotional up-set. She's going to need someone with her for weeks, if not months. And that someone is obviously me.'

'She's lucky to have such a devoted sister.' His voice was flat, matter-of-fact. It made what he said seem more sincere.

Hers was equally toneless. 'I know she'd do the same for me.'

'It's good to know there is such love around.' For a moment he appeared to be thinking of something else. But then he went on, 'Now, if you're serious about looking for a job, I know the nursing manager for the A and E department. Her name's Margaret Welsh, she's the mother of my practice manager. She's a bit of a dragon, but she gets things done. I could have a word, if you like. You should be able to get on the Bank.'

'I'd like that.' The Bank was a system whereby qualified but unemployed nurses could work when hospitals were short of staff. In these days, when staffing levels were cut to the minimum, there was always work to be had. She knew that working on the Bank would mean that she would be offered all the unsocial hours that other nurses didn't want, would be expected to come to work at a few hours' notice, would rarely be able to plan more than a couple of days ahead. But she'd be at the same hospital as her sister.

Steve seemed to relax. 'I'm glad you can stay,' he said, 'it'll certainly make a lot of difference to Jo's recovery. But is there no man waiting for you in Las Vegas? No one expecting you back?'

She laughed. 'I've got a lot of male friends but no one in particular. In fact there is one waiting—in spite of everything I've told him. He's more interested in me than I am in him. It's a bit awkward, really. I like him and I don't want to hurt him. But he's not the man for me.'

'I'm glad you feel you can stay,' he said. He was silent for a few minutes, and then he went on. 'You know, the only times I've been with you there's been some kind of emergency. We've never talked like ordinary people. I'm off on a course down south for a week, but when I get back perhaps we could have a drink sometimes, and just chat.'

'Sounds good,' she said. After a pause, she added, 'I think I'd really like that'.

Kate knew how much the mind could affect the body. As the doctor had said in A and E, Jo's injury was serious, but not life-threatening. There would be a week or so of pain and discomfort in hospital, then home rest, recuperation and some physiotherapy. But the combination of emotional stress and the broken leg was not a good one. When she visited Jo next morning in hospital she found her sister listless and weepy in turn.

'I'm staying,' she told her. 'I'm fed up with the States, and I'm staying here for some months. Getting a job, in fact.'

The good news did please her sister. 'Kate! You're doing that for me?'

'Certainly not,' Kate said, lying valiantly. 'I'm doing it for me. I like the room you've given me, and I fancy working in England for a change. And in my spare time I'll keep an eye on you.'

In fact she was half wondering if it was necessary. Jo obviously had plenty of friends. Her little side room was full of flowers and get-well cards, and there had been no end of calls. People might not know quite how to respond to the news of a cancelled wedding, but they certainly knew what to do when a friend had broken her leg.

She stayed a little longer, and then left. Jo needed to sleep. As she walked down the corridor she was momentarily silhouetted against a high window, the sun shining in on her. And a voice boomed out, 'Jo, are you mad? What are you doing out of bed?'

She turned. Striding towards her was a tall man carrying a bunch of roses; he was in his fifties, with surprisingly long blond hair. 'I heard you had broken your…' Then he saw her properly. 'Good Lord, you're not Jo. I'm sorry. You must be Kate, the twin sister I've heard so much about.' He thrust out his hand. 'I'm Andrew Kirk. My daughters were going to be bridesmaids with you.'

'I've heard a lot about you too, Mr Kirk,' she said. 'It's good to meet you at last.'

'I take it you've been to see Jo. How is she?'

'She'll survive,' Kate said briefly.

Andrew was shrewd; he caught the unspoken message at once. 'That bad, is it? Emotional and physical trauma—not a good combination. I'm a neurologist; I know as much as anyone about cutting up brains. But we still know far too little about the mind.'

He was subjecting her to an intense inspection, but she didn't really mind. 'Are you as good a nurse as your sister?' he demanded.

'Yes,' she said simply. 'But I work in A and E, not the theatre.'

'Confident too?'

'Confident but not over-confident. When things need doing in A and E, they often need doing fast.'

'An excellent philosophy—for A and E that is. What are your future plans?'

'I'm staying here as long as my sister needs me, and that might be some time. I think I'll apply for a job on the Bank and see if there's work in A and E.'

'Good. I can't be a referee for you, but if anyone

asks me I'll say I think you'll be an asset to the hospital. I'll be in touch, Kate.'

Then he was on his way. Kate blinked.

'No Lucy, I don't know how long I'll stay over here….my sister Jo is in a bit of a state; she needs me. I'm going to try to get a job.'

Lucy in Las Vegas sounded as clear as if she was phoning from the next room. 'So you want me to let your room, store your stuff and just send on the personal bits out of the top two drawers?'

'That's it, I guess. Sorry to put you to this trouble, Lucy, and I'll pay the room rent until it's let.'

'No trouble and no need,' Lucy drawled. 'I'm sorry about your sister and we're going to miss you. But in fact things have worked out well. Harvey and me— well, we've finally got it together. I've got a rock for my finger, so he can move his stuff into your room. And you make sure you're over here when we get married!'

'It's a promise, Lucy. Nothing will stop me. What's the weather like out there?'

'It's a hot one. We're hitting a hundred. How about you?'

'We're going to have a hot one too. It's supposed to be going up to sixty-five.'

Lucy laughed. 'You'd better put on your flannel undershirt. Hey, listen, does John the surgeon know that you're not going to come back?'

Kate winced. 'Not yet. In fact he's the next call.'

'Good luck, kid. Make him phone you back. Because you know he's going to be on the line for hours.'

Lucy rang off, and Kate sat for a minute thinking. She had lived in Las Vegas for three years now—the longest she had stayed any where since she had started wandering. There was so much to do and see there. And yet she had managed to cut off her life there with one phone call. Were there many people her age with so few possessions, so few roots? Did she intend to lead this kind of life indefinitely? Suddenly it didn't seem as exciting as it once had. Was it time to settle down?

She pushed the question to the back of her mind. She had other things to do.

She phoned John. John, predictably, was scandalised, horrified, amazed. She knew he was all of these; he told her so. 'But what about *us*?' he exploded. 'You can't just leave things like that.'

'John, I've told you, there is no us. We're friends—good friends, I hope. If I ever get back I'll look forward to seeing you again.'

Once again, predictably, John paid no attention to what she said. 'What about the chance of training for the emergency response team?' he demanded. 'You'll lose it if you're not here.'

Now that did hurt. She had seen her future in emergency nursing, had been looking forward both to the training and the work. But her sister came first. 'I'll just have to lose the chance, won't I?' she said. 'Some decisions in life are hard.'

Now John decided to be understanding—again. Adopting a solicitous voice, he said, 'You're upset; I can tell that. Just don't make any hasty decisions. There's no need yet. I'll ask if they can keep a place open for you on the team. And, remember, I'm here for you. What's your number? I'll phone you.'

She had carefully dialled 141 before phoning him; she knew if once he had her number he'd be on the phone at all times. 'Don't worry, I'm out a lot. I'll ring you in a couple of days. Got to go now, John, I'm being interviewed for a job at the Milner Hospital in a couple of minutes.'

This last was a lie, but John would go on if he wasn't cut short. She put down the phone, feeling warm. Why didn't she think more of John? she asked herself. He was definitely a catch. He was good-looking, had an excellent career in front of him, and, although at times he tended to fuss a bit, she knew that underneath he was a good-hearted man. I just couldn't love him, she decided.

She sighed and stretched, walked to the front window and peered out at the estate of new houses, the fields of the valley below. She had made her decision now. She was staying in Kirkhelen—well, for the foreseeable future. For a moment her mind went back to the lights of Las Vegas, to the constant social life, to the mountain-walking. Then she smiled. She was happy to be here. The next step was to get work.

Fortunately, this was not too hard. It only took five days. Before she had gone to Vegas she had worked for some months in London, so her registration was still valid. There were people in Liverpool who remembered her from her training days, and they gave her an excellent reference. She got another reference—faxed from Las Vegas. She knew how hospitals worked, and suspected that Andrew Kirk had had a quiet word with someone.

Finally she was interviewed by the A and E nursing manager, Margaret Welsh. Kate wasn't immediately struck by her friendliness. The woman held herself very erect, her hair pulled back painfully tightly into a bun. She was old enough to remember the old days, when sisters had had absolute power over their nurses, and Kate suspected that she viewed the passing of those days with regret. The woman was obviously very competent, however; her questions showed that. Kate was taken through her training, questioned closely on the work she had done in America, and asked if she thought she could make the transition from American to English practice. 'There's no great difference,' Kate said.

'You understand we can't guarantee you regular work? You can't expect just to walk in and pick and choose?'

'I've no intention of doing so. I'll be very grateful for whatever you can offer me.'

This submissive answer seemed to satisfy Mrs Welsh. 'We'll give you a trial, then. In fact, if it works out well, we have a nurse who's going to be off for the next ten days. You can take her shifts if you like.'

'I'd like that very much.'

'In that case I'll show you round right now. You can start on Monday.'

She felt instantly at home when she walked in on Monday night, wearing her new uniform. There was so little difference between the American Emergency Room and the English A and E Department. She had been shown round, given a talk on what the department expected from her, and now she was expected to get on with it.

And the first person she met was Steve! He was in a white coat, stethoscope round his neck, and he looked very pleased to see her.

'Steve! What are you doing here?'

'Working,' he told her. 'We can talk later, but right

now we've got some suturing to do in that cubicle there. Think you could find me a suture trolley?'

There were questions she wanted to ask, things she wanted to say, but she too was here to work. 'Be right with you,' she said. She had memorised the positions of most of what she might be asked to fetch.

The patient was a middle-aged man whose cement-covered clothes suggested that he had been working on a building site. He was lying on the stretcher, the left leg of his trousers cut to the thigh. Round his calf was wrapped a very amateurish bandage and blood was seeping through it.

Carefully Kate started to cut away the bandage as Steve introduced himself and asked how the accident had happened.

'My own fault,' the man panted. 'I couldn't be bothered to wait for someone to help me. We're working late, and everyone's in a bit of a hurry. I picked up this sheet of corrugated iron and tried to throw it on the back of the lorry. It was too heavy and it slipped. A jagged edge caught my leg. The foreman's going to kill me. He thinks he's going to get the blame for accidents.'

'Somebody should take responsibility,' Steve said. 'Are your tetanus jabs up to date?'

'Yes. The firm insists on that.'

Kate eased away the last bandage and there was a sudden gush of bright red blood. She pushed her fingers tight over the gash. 'Arterial bleeding, Steve!'

'We're going to need arterial forceps,' he said calmly.

It was work she had done often before. She liked working with Steve, found herself getting into a rhythm with him; she could anticipate what he was going to need. This kind of unspoken partnership she had developed before, with other doctors, but never so quickly as she did with Steve. They would make a good team.

They finished the suturing and Steve decided to admit the man, at least overnight. Then the two of them were called urgently to see to Lizzie Collis, a seventeen-year-old who had taken an overdose of paracetamol. Steve eased in a tube to protect the airway while Kate prepared to wash out the stomach.

'Why do they do it?' he whispered to Kate. 'I gather it's boyfriend trouble. All right, this might be a gesture—but she might have done herself serious damage. The things paracetamol can do to the liver don't bear thinking about.'

Kate thought of her own sister. 'Perhaps Lizzie here thought she was in love,' she snapped, 'and love makes people do stupid things. With any luck she'll recover from this, and know better in future.'

Steve looked at her, surprised at her vehemence. 'You could be right,' he said. 'But don't forget that love can make people do wonderful things too. Now, d'you want to find out if there's a bed vacant in Women's Medical for Lizzie? Then perhaps we can steal a coffee.'

Somehow, three o'clock in the morning didn't seem a strange time to be talking to him. There was an intimacy in the bare little staff room, with its uncomfortable chairs and the drinks machine, that made everything, hot or cold, taste of plastic. 'You haven't explained what you're doing here,' she said. 'You're supposed to be a GP.'

'I am a GP. If you remember, I told you that I'd be doing some work in the A and E Department here. This is part of it.'

She did remember. It was when they had first met.

'And did you arrange to work here when you knew I would be on duty?' she asked suspiciously.

He shook his head. 'I didn't know you'd be working this shift until this afternoon. But I'm glad we're together; I think you're a good nurse. You know to do things without being told. D'you mind if I try to arrange to work with you again? I can organise the times when I come in.'

'I'd like that,' she said. His compliment pleased her no end. 'D'you think that we...?'

An orderly poked her head round the door. 'Ambulance coming. Sounds like a heart attack.'

'Back to work,' said Steve.

'So, how did you find your first shift in an English hospital?' Steve grinned.

It was morning. Soon she would be able to go home and sleep. 'Hard,' she said promptly. 'Very similar to America, though. In fact, the biggest difference between here and Las Vegas is that everyone here seems to speak English. An awful lot of patients over there speak Mexican or Spanish as their first language. There are many immigrants in Las Vegas.'

'So how do you cope?'

'I've picked up a fair amount of Spanish. Otherwise, we call in an interpreter.'

He grimaced. 'That must make things really hard. What other differences are there? In the programmes I've seen on TV, all the doctors seem to be handsome young men and all the nurses unflappable beauties.'

'That is perfectly correct,' she told him. 'You can't practise medicine in America unless you're a perfect physical specimen.' Then she grinned too.

'Must make it difficult for some,' he said. 'What are you doing now?'

'Going up to see Jo. She seems to be coming along. Are you on tonight, Steve?'

'Sadly not. But I've enjoyed working with you, Kate. Somehow I knew you'd be a good nurse. It's good to have your feelings shown to be right.'

'We're a good team,' she said.

Kate was weary. The first shift had taken it out of her, but she had expected it to. First time on nights was always a shock. But she was happy too. She had enjoyed her work, and she had been made to feel welcome. Doctors, nurses and technicians all worked well together.

She had learned a bit more about Steve too. Not just that he was a good doctor—she had suspected that anyway. The danger with working in A and E, with the rapid through-put of patients, was that you tended to see cases, not people. In the turbulence of the moment, even the best of A and E doctors would think of the greenstick fracture to the humerus in room C, rather than of five-year-old frightened Ben Johnson, who wanted his mother.

But not Steve. Perhaps it was because of his work as a GP, but for him the patient as a person always came first.

It was going to be a hot day—for England. She strode through the grounds, enjoying the early-morning sunshine. It struck her that if she had been walking in her Las Vegas hospital she would have been moving through air-conditioned corridors, the sun kept well at bay. None of the wards in the Milner were air-conditioned. It seemed odd.

She always managed to get in to see Jo two or three times a day. There were a lot of other visitors, but Jo seemed to look forward to her visits most. 'I don't have to pretend with you,' she said today. 'If I want to be miserable, I can be.'

'I don't want you to be miserable,' Kate said. 'You know it'll be a while before you can work again. Why don't you study something—find something to occupy your mind?' She indicated the pile of unread books and magazines on the bedside cabinet. 'This lot doesn't seem to be doing too much for you.'

'I'll decide on something in a while,' Jo said listlessly. 'Tell me how your first night was.'

'It was hard, but I enjoyed it. I remember when you used to enjoy hard work, Jo.'

She must have been more tired than she knew. She hadn't intended to say such a hurtful thing. But Jo didn't seem to notice. 'I'll get back to work in time,' she said.

CHAPTER FOUR

KATE slept well during the day, which she hadn't expected. Usually, the first couple of days' sleep after coming off nights were disturbed and short. But not this time. Not that she felt entirely refreshed. That would be too much to ask.

She was sitting downstairs, in the late afternoon, having her first coffee of the day, when the phone rang. The voice that spoke was steely, efficient, but not very friendly. 'Is that Miss Wilde?'

'This is Kate Wilde. Do you want to speak to my sister Jo?' Kate was aware that she was not in her own house.

'No, it's you that we want. This is Vanessa Welsh, practice manager for Dr Russell.'

'Vanessa? Oh, great, I've been meaning to ring you to thank you for what you did to help my sister. We were both…'

The voice interrupted. 'I am happy to help Dr Russell and his patients in any way I can. That is what I see as my job. Could you hold? He wishes to talk to you.' There was no time for an answer, just a click and then a low buzzing.

In fact she had to wait quite a long time before he finally did speak. But when she heard his voice she felt a sudden burst of joy. And she'd only parted from him eight hours ago! Still, she mustn't let him know how she felt. Not yet, anyway.

'Kate! I hope I didn't wake you. How d'you feel after your first night shift?'

She laughed. 'I've recovered slightly. But what are you doing at work? Why aren't you sleeping too?'

'A GP's bookwork never stops. I had a few hours in bed then came in to look at some papers.'

It was exciting just to chat to him. She knew that her cheeks were slightly flushed. Still... 'What's the idea of getting your practice manager to phone me?' she asked. 'Why didn't you phone direct?'

'Sorry, Kate. It's Vanessa's idea. All calls should be routed through the switchboard. It's supposed to save me time. She's been on one of these courses for efficiency and time-saving for practices. Look, Kate, I need a favour. Are you free next Saturday or Sunday?'

She thought a moment. 'I'm going in early on Saturday night—apparently it's always busy. But I'm not working Sunday night because I'm due to start work on days on Monday. So if I get a couple of hours' sleep early on Sunday morning, I could be free then.' She guessed he'd accept this, knowing that nurses, like doctors, had to get used to doing without sleep. 'Why, what do you want?'

'Well, I'll keep it as a bit of a surprise for you, but it could turn into a sort of walk and lunch. I'll show you some of the moors to the north of here. I might need a nurse for what I've got in mind, and I can't really ask the practice nurse. In fact I think I want a friend, rather than a nurse.'

'Sounds intriguing. I'd love to come. But what do I wear and shall I bring anything to do with nursing?'

'I'll bring any medical stuff. Just you bring your boots and sweater. Pick you up at about half past eleven?'

'That'll be fine. Shall I put up some sandwiches?'

'No...we can have a pub meal. Looking forward to seeing you, Kate.'

'Me likewise.' She rang off. Great, she was going out with Steve. It struck her that her life so far in England had been all hard work and suffering. But she ought to be able to enjoy herself for a while. She was really looking forward to her outing with Steve.

A few days later, Sunday morning found her in Steve's car, heading for the Lancashire moors. He was explaining where they were going.

'Mrs Branwell—Amy—is eighty-seven,' Steve told her. 'I've known her all my life. Her husband Jack was a biology teacher who did an awful lot to get me into medical school. I had extra lessons at their house, and Amy always used to come in with a plate of home-baked biscuits. She's a kind woman—in fact they were a very kind couple.

'Anyway, Jack retired about twenty years ago. They bought this cottage up on the moors. Jack had always been a great gardener and gardening was how he wanted to spend the rest of his life. I felt I owed them both a lot, so I kept in touch through medical school and ever since. Jack died five years ago. I've kept in touch with Amy, but things have been a bit difficult lately and I haven't been to see her for quite a few months. But I got in touch with her GP and told him that if there was anything I could do, would he please phone me. Well, he's just done that.'

'They had no children?' Kate asked.

'No children,' he confirmed. 'Perhaps that's why he was such a good teacher. Pity, really, they would have been wonderful parents. Anyhow, earlier this week the

GP—a Dr Stanmore—did phone me. He said that Amy was getting more and more frail, that she couldn't really look after herself, and he wanted her to move into sheltered accommodation. But, typically, she's being awkward. He just wondered if I could persuade her.'

'He sounds like a good GP,' Kate said. 'He seems to know his patients.'

'I think he is a good GP. And I suspect he knows that it's not going to be easy to change Amy's mind.'

'So where do I fit in?' asked Kate. 'What do you need a nurse for?'

Steve looked a little uncomfortable. 'Well, she might need some kind of attention. Nursing attention, I mean. And, no matter what I think is wrong with her, I can't see myself being allowed to do anything but the rank minimum. Don't forget, she still sees me as an embarrassed and blushing sixth-former.'

'I bet you were a lovely six-former,' giggled Kate, 'and I'd love to see you blushing and embarrassed.'

'Not a pretty sight. And there was another reason for asking you along.' He turned to glance at her.

'The other reason being?'

'I wanted to spend some time with you.'

She thought about this for a moment, and then said, 'That's nice. And I'm glad you asked me out. I'm enjoying myself already.'

They had just moved off the motorway and were heading towards the Pendle hills. She liked this area, the green, smooth-topped hills, the crazily wandering white stone walls. And it was a good day for visiting—warm, but with a breeze.

He was wearing fawn chinos and a white T-shirt. It was an outfit that flattered a man, but only if he had the necessary figure for it. And Steve had that figure. There was no hint of a thickening waist, and the muscles of his arms and neck showed brown against the whiteness. He didn't look like her idea of a GP—the dark suit, white shirt, sober tie—though she knew he could dress that way if he needed to.

She was dressed similarly casually, in a blue shirt and a pair of jeans. Both of them wore trainers, and there were boots in bags behind them, and also sweaters and waterproofs. She and Steve were alike in so many ways, she thought. Not like her and John. The intrusive thought popped out. Feeling rather uncomfortable at the thought, she asked Steve what their programme was.

'I thought we'd call at the GP's house first; he said to come at any time. Then we'll go round to see Amy and afterwards perhaps have a walk. If you'd like a walk, that is.'

'I would. I really would.' She paused a minute, and then said, 'I love my sister, but now I feel I need to get away from the hurt and damage of the past few weeks. I want just a few hours to myself. D'you think that's selfish?'

Quietly, he said, 'No one could call you selfish. You should know that if it hadn't been for you Jo would have been in a far worse state. You've been a tremendous support to her.'

'She'd do the same for me, you know. I've not done anything special.'

'You're wrong. As a GP, I see a lot of families in stressed situations. Some cope magnificently. An awful lot don't. You and Jo have got something that's valuable.'

They drove on in happy silence for a few more minutes. She had her window open and was enjoying the air. Since leaving the motorway he had slowed down considerably, and it made the journey a lot more pleasant. There was time to look around.

After a while she turned to look at Steve. He was frowning, as if he had a problem. She knew he had glanced at her once or twice, as if to start saying something, but he still remained silent.

'Come on,' she said. 'You're trying to tell me something but you don't know how. Let me guess. You've forgotten your wallet and I'll have to pay for everything.'

He laughed. 'Nothing as straightforward as that. Just something that I think perhaps you ought to know.'

'Go on,' she said, intrigued, 'tell me your guilty secret.'

'We-e-ell. It's not really a secret. Did you know that some years ago I took Jo out for a while? In fact we were quite—involved?'

This was really interesting, even a bit alarming. 'No,' she said, 'I didn't know that. Though Jo once said that she'd have married you if it wasn't for Harry. I thought it was just a joke. What happened?'

'Well, it was just before she met Harry. In fact, I suppose it was through me that she did meet him. We went out for quite a while, and then Harry came along—and that was it. I couldn't stand in the way of true love.'

'There's a bit of bitterness creeping in there,' she said. 'Did you feel bad about losing Jo to Harry?'

He shrugged. 'I suppose so, yes. But I was working very hard and I put off telling Jo how I felt. It looked like a very casual relationship and I thought there was plenty of time for it to develop.'

Kate thought about this for a while. She wondered if there had been more to the attraction than he was willing to tell her. 'If it had been you and not Harry she'd stayed with,' she said, 'then all this wouldn't have happened.'

She felt instantly guilty at the thought that followed this. She didn't want to think of Jo and Steve happily together. She wanted Steve to be free to...

'Thinking about what might have happened is pointless,' he said. 'Look, see that hill over there? Behind the crest is where Amy lives.' His voice was brusque.

'You can't change the subject now, Steve,' she said gently. 'It's been brought up; we have to think about it. Do you think...do you wonder...in the future perhaps there might be some hope for you and Jo getting together again?'

'No!' The word was curt, final. Kate made no reply, and after a while he apparently realised that he had to say something more. 'I feel a lot for Jo. But over the past few weeks I've been helping with this marriage, pretending that I was delighted, and I've come to accept that Jo is not for me. I can't go back on that.'

'That I can understand.' Kate felt relieved, but she didn't want to show it. She hesitated, then asked. 'Does Jo know how much she's hurt you?'

She was pleased that he didn't deny he had been hurt. 'I don't think so,' he said. 'It was only a light-hearted affair at first. I was working like mad and I thought things would be all right until... Then Harry came along and swept her off her feet. I was wrong, wasn't I?'

'We all make mistakes.' There was another question she knew she had to ask and she wasn't sure she wanted to know the answer. Although she was sitting, apparently relaxed in the car, she could feel her heart pounding. For a couple of minutes she waited, and then, 'Steve, I want an honest answer. In spite of what you say, I think you still feel something for Jo. What do you feel for me? To you, am I Kate Wilde, a person in my own right, or am I just a copy of a girl you once loved?'

She turned to look at him. There was the faint sheen of sweat on his forehead, though it was quite cool in the car. It was quite some time before he answered, but then, 'You and Jo are vastly different in character. And when I look at you, it's Kate I see, not Jo. Now, can we talk about something else? I know it might be necessary, but I'm not enjoying this conversation.'

She leaned over to kiss him on the cheek. 'Neither am I. Let's get back to being friends on a day out in the country.' But she knew the conversation would come back to haunt her.

They drove further down the valley and into Bramley, a little grey-stone village. The GP had said his house was at the far end, and they found him in his garden. Dr Stanmore was an elderly man, but his eyes were shrewd and his manner calm.

'Good, you've given me an excuse to stop work,' he said. 'Come and sit in the shade and I'll fetch us all a lemonade.' He led them to a little tree-lined arbour.

The lemonade turned out to be home-made, thick and tart. Kate had to add a little sugar to hers, and then found it amazingly refreshing.

The doctors got on at once. There was a little general medical talk, the usual grumble about government funding cuts, and then they considered Amy Branwell.

'She mustn't stay up there another winter,' said Dr Stanmore. 'Apart from anything else, there's going to be days when she'll be cut off by snow. If we have a bad winter it could be weeks. And I don't want her bounced down the track in a skidding Land Rover.'

'That place has been her life for the past twenty

years,' Steve said. 'It has memories for her. She won't move easily.'

'I know that. She told me she wanted to die there—I told her that there was no good reason to die yet. For a person her age she's very sound.' Dr Stanmore frowned. 'There's a very good retirement home here in the village called Pendle View. Run by an ex-matron; I've known her all my life. It has a great view, and the grounds run down to the river at the back. In another few years I'll reserve myself a place. I know Amy would be happy there—but she just won't try it.'

Steve nodded. 'We'll drive up there and have a word. I used to have a bit of influence with her—but you know she can be stubborn.'

'I know that. But I'm fond of Amy—I played chess with her and her husband. I'd like to get her sorted out for his sake. I've asked the district nurse to look in on her from time to time, but she's very busy already. It's a long way to go and she just can't call all that often. If you have any success—let me know.'

'I'll do so happily. Nice to have met you, Dr Stanmore. We'll be in touch.'

They drove slowly though the village. 'Fancy a pub meal for lunch?' he asked, nodding at an attractive-looking building on their right. 'They're advertising food.'

She hesitated a minute. Amy Branwell was his friend, he ought to make the decisions, but... 'I saw a food shop a little way back,' she said. 'It looked like a high-class place, home-made pies and salads and stuff. Would it be all right if we took a picnic up to Amy's? Then she could join us—if you don't think she might be upset.'

'I think that's a great idea! You're sure you wouldn't mind? I mean, having a picnic rather than a proper meal?'

'Of course not! Anyway, from what I could see it seemed quite a classy sort of place.'

'Let's go then.' He pulled the car round in a U-turn.

It *was* quite a classy little place. There was a wonderful selection of cheeses for a start, and a variety of made-up salads, beautifully crusty pies. When he saw that they were making a generous selection, the proprietor gave them a basket to hold everything. Last of all Steve added a bottle of white wine. 'It'll do for the middle of the day,' he told her. 'It's quite light and we'll enjoy just a glass each.'

Then they set off again. For the first two miles they followed the main road, but then they turned onto the narrowest of minor roads and chugged slowly upwards. Fortunately nothing came down towards them, there was only room for one vehicle. Finally the road just stopped. Kate got out and opened a gate, and then they took a track to the shoulder of the hill.

They moved even more slowly. It was difficult enough driving on a dry surface in summer, and she wondered what it would be like in winter. Probably almost impassable. But they lurched ever upwards, and eventually reached Amy's home.

Steve stopped the car by the front gate, and she stepped out and turned, just looking. The view took Kate's breath away. The cottage had obviously once been a farm, and was built under the shelter of a little rock outcrop. All around she could see for miles. There was the village they had left some twenty minutes before, and to the other side she could see the distant sea.

He put a companionable arm round her shoulders.

'Quite something, isn't it?' he said. 'I've spent hours just looking at this view.'

'I can see why someone would never want to move from here.'

He sighed. 'Sometimes decisions have to be made and you have to move on in life. Let's go and find Amy.' They walked down to the front door.

The garden was large and had obviously once been lovingly cared for. But now it was showing signs of neglect; weeds were getting a hold. The house too needed minor maintenance. She saw an overflowing gutter, a slightly rotted windowframe.

Steve had to knock twice before Amy appeared. Then the door opened. 'Steve, it's you! How wonderful to see you.' He wrapped his arms round the delighted old lady and kissed her affectionately.

Amy wore a floral dress, with two pairs of glasses hung round her neck. She was getting old now, her skin had a thin, translucent look and her white hair was sparse. But the high cheekbones showed that once she had been a beauty, and there was intelligence still in the limpid grey eyes.

'And you've brought a young lady to meet me. That's kind. I don't get many visitors.'

'Amy, this is Kate Wilde. She's a nurse and a very good friend of mine.'

Amy's grip was firm. 'I like medical people, Kate,' she said. 'Now, both of you come in.'

It was a comfortable living room, slightly shabby but lived in. Two walls were lined with bookcases, and pictures largely covered the rest of the walls. A rocking chair was drawn up to the fireplace.

For a six-month period Kate had once worked with a district nurse. She'd had to assess the health—mental and physical—of her clients, often without being able to examine them. It had become second nature when walking into a new home to look round for the signs of neglect. Amy was obviously house-proud. But Kate noticed the dust on the picture rail, the spilled matches by the gas fire. Amy wasn't as fit as perhaps she thought.

'We brought a picnic with us,' Steve said. 'We thought perhaps you'd join us.' He dropped the basket on the table.

'That would be so nice! I was just about to boil myself an egg. But I'll make us a cup of tea and then we'll catch up on the news.'

'Why don't I make the tea?' Kate asked. 'And you can have longer talking to Steve.'

Amy smiled at her gently. 'If you wish, dear,' she said, and Kate was well aware that the old lady knew *exactly* what she was thinking. She took the basket and walked along a passage and into the kitchen.

There were more signs—not exactly of neglect, but of difficulty in the kitchen. When Kate wanted to warm the pies she found the top half of the oven spotless, but in the back of the bottom half there was an obviously forgotten casserole dish, with something still in it. Amy couldn't reach or see the tops of her cupboards and the doors were grimy. Kate put on the kettle and laid out a tray, then ran round the kitchen trying to clean what she could.

Next door to the kitchen was the bathroom. Kate slipped in to look round. There was no shower, and when she felt the bottom of the bath it too was dusty. Amy hadn't had a bath for four or five weeks. Not sure whether to feel like a Peeping Tom, Kate went back to the kitchen and did a little more cleaning.

A while later she took the meal into the living room.

Steve and Amy were sitting side by side, poring over books and old photograph albums. 'Look here,' Amy said gleefully, 'do you recognise this young man?'

She showed Kate an old school magazine. There was a full-page picture of a cricket team, and in the middle was the captain—a cheerfully smiling Steve. His hair was longer and his face much younger but the smile was the same. 'Isn't he sweet?' Kate asked.

Amy laughed while Steve looked gloomy. 'Who would have thought that that sweet young man could turn into sour old me?' he asked.

'You're not sour,' she told him. 'You're just... mature.'

There was an oak gate-legged table beside the wall. Kate pulled it out and the three of them sat down to what she had prepared. Kate noticed that Amy ate heartily—and wondered when the old lady had last had such a substantial meal. When they had finished Kate cleared away the dishes, and then said, 'Why don't you go for a wander round the garden, Steve? Amy and I could have a little chat—you know, women's talk.' She turned. 'Would you like that, Amy?'

'After that meal I'll agree to everything you want,' Amy said serenely. 'Well, nearly everything.'

Steve looked at the two of them thoughtfully, then said, 'I think I'm outnumbered here.' He walked outside.

'Now, tell me all about yourself,' Amy said. 'Steve was saying you've just come back from Las Vegas. What's it like there? I'd love to go.'

They chatted generally for a while, and then Kate crossed her fingers behind her back and said, 'Amy, you know I'm a nurse. I was wondering if...if you'd like me to help you have a bath. I know you can do it your-self, but...'

Amy looked at her sharp-eyed. 'I'm not a fool, you know,' she said. 'I hear what you're saying and I know what you're thinking. You think I'm not able to look after myself.'

Kate pointed to the opened school magazine, with the picture of the younger Steve. 'Everyone needs help some time,' she said. 'Steve told me how much you and your husband helped him when he was at school. He...would like to repay that help a little.'

There was a pause, then, 'All right,' Amy said. 'I must say it's a bit hard climbing in and out of the bath. Mind you, you can do marvels with a hot flannel!'

'Her brain is as good as ever,' Steve said. 'She still gets books sent up from the library, and complains that there aren't enough scientific books in large print. But her body's letting her down, and she won't face up to it.'

'Better to be that way than to give up entirely,' Kate said.

'Is she fit to be left on her own? You had the chance of a longer conversation than I did. How d'you think she's coping?'

Kate marshalled her thoughts. 'At the moment she's coping—but only just. And she doesn't want to move. Trying to force her into anything she doesn't want would be terrible.'

'I think I agree with you.'

They were driving away from Amy's cottage. They had decided not to stay too long—they wanted to have a walk even if it was a short one. But Amy had made Steve promise to come again quite soon, and to bring Kate with him.

'I liked her a lot,' Kate said. 'She obviously still loves and misses her husband. She talked about him when she was having a bath. Why did they not have children?'

Steve shrugged. 'I guess it just didn't happen. These days we might have been able to do something—we forget how rapidly we've progressed with fertility treatment. If I'd been a hospital doctor instead of a GP, that's the kind of work I would have liked to do.'

'It's a pity. I think they would have been wonderful parents. Now, where are you taking me?'

'I promised you a walk. This will be nothing like the Grand Canyon, but I think you'll like it.'

They drove back into the village, parked and put on their boots. She brought out her tube of sunblock, insisted that he smear it over his face, then they set off. For a while they walked along a well-trodden path by the side of the river. Then he led her up a path that cut across the side of the hill, climbing steadily but with a very reasonable gradient. Nearer the top of the hill the path degenerated into a track and got steeper. But she was determined not to slow down. She copied his easy, mountaineer's pace until they finally climbed up onto the ridge. There was a view like the one by Amy's cottage. They could see for miles.

Both of them were breathing heavily, and they paused for a moment. 'Worth the effort?' he asked her.

'It's always worth the effort. Look, you can see the Cumbrian Fells.'

After that they followed the ridge, gently climbing and descending, along a great arc. The footing was easy on the sheep-cropped grass and they walked side by side, enjoying themselves, sweaters tied round their waists. It was warm, but a gentle breeze made the air feel blissful. And they had the fells to themselves. They could see for miles, not another person in sight.

After a while the breeze dropped, and Steve stopped to take off his shirt. 'Sunblock time again,' Kate shouted, feeling in her little rucksack for the tube. 'Turn your back to me.'

He grinned. 'You're very particular. Afraid of skin cancer—melanoma?'

'You *never* walk around Las Vegas without sunblock,' she told him. 'The number of people we've had in the Emergency Room who think that they're tough and hard—the sun won't hurt them. I once spent an entire day sponging down a man whose temperature had rocketed. He was very fair-skinned, had just flown in from the East Coast, and told me he thought sunblock was for what he called wimps. Did he learn different!'

Steve held up his hands. 'I give in. You may sunblock my back.'

But when she started it was strangely difficult. She squeezed the cream onto her hands and started to rub across the top of his shoulders. Places where the bone was near the skin were danger spots. His skin was warm, and she found herself stroking rather than rubbing. Under her fingertips the muscles felt firm and alive; she could feel the great swell of his latissimus dorsi, the curve of his deltoids, the twin pillars at each side of his spine. 'That's nice,' he said softly.

She had enjoyed it too, but she didn't want him to think so. Thrusting the tube at him, she said abruptly, 'You can do your chest yourself.'

It *was* warm. Now the breeze had dropped she could feel her own T-shirt clinging to her. Well, they were friends, weren't they? He wouldn't mind. Before she had a chance to change her mind, she crossed her arms in front of her and pulled off the sticky garment, standing there in her white serviceable bra. 'That *is* better,' she said. 'Now you can put sunblock on my back.'

At first his fingers were firmer than hers had been; she decided they were the fingers of a doctor. But then they slowed, and she knew without a doubt that he was caressing her as a lover would. To him she was a woman, not a patient. And she loved it.

When she managed to speak her voice sounded strained. 'Perhaps we'd better walk on now?'

His voice was equally hoarse. 'Perhaps we had.' Both recognised that now was not the time. But the time would come.

Five minutes later any slight embarrassment either of them might have felt had disappeared. She realised how long it had been since she had walked like this and how much she had missed it. He appeared to feel the same. It was good to talk to a good-looking man who was a kindred spirit.

'I've walked all over Europe,' he told her, 'but never in America. What's the walking like over there?'

'Fantastic. I can't describe it. Just come over some time and I'll show you.'

'So you are going back? You seemed to leave very easily. You said there was no job or flat or man waiting for you?'

'I've got a lot of friends there. But in general I like to travel light; I don't like being tied down. I'll go back some time, and I might stay a while longer, or I might wander on.' This was a speech she had made before. She wondered if it was now sounding just a bit glib.

'You're not like Jo, are you? You're much more a free spirit. I admire someone who is tough enough to enjoy life and walk through it without commitments.'

She was not sure she was pleased about this comment. 'I have got commitments,' she pointed out. 'Well, one big one—that's my sister. Mind you, I tend to love her from a distance. And when I am doing a job I quickly get committed to that too.'

He didn't reply at once. Then, 'Having one big commitment is a lot more dangerous than having a few lesser ones. I think it's madness to invest all your happiness in just one person. Look at what happened to Jo. I think your idea is best—find a man you like, leave him when you like. I think friendly, casual relationships are best.'

She hadn't expected this! 'You know nothing about the way I view men,' she told him tartly. 'The only relationship you know about is the fact that I told you there's a man in America who wants to see more of me than I really want.'

'I can sympathise with him,' Steve said, and she felt rather pleased.

They walked on for a while, and then she said thoughtfully, 'Are you giving me your own view of what relationships should be like? It sounded that way to me.'

This time the silence was even longer, and she wondered if he was going to reply. Then, 'Yes, I suppose I was giving my own view.'

'I know you're not married,' Kate said, 'and we've talked about Jo. Apart from her, were you never tempted?'

'I was tempted once. I didn't fall.'

'Was it you that didn't fall—or did the woman in question decide that it wasn't a good idea?'

He looked at her in astonishment a moment, and then laughed. 'Kate, you're too perceptive. And you're absolutely right. Yes, it was her idea that we didn't get married. Her name was Madeleine. In fact she married someone older, but also an awful lot richer than me. Three years afterwards she phoned me, said life was fine for her but that she got a bit bored at times. Perhaps we could take up what we had again, meet on occasions for—whatever.'

'But even wanting only casual relationships you said no?'

'You guessed right,' he admitted.

'Why? It sounds is if it had everything you wanted.'

He turned to her, perplexed. 'First of all, you answer me a question,' he said. 'Why am I telling you all this when I've never told anyone else?'

She answered promptly. 'Because I'm your friend,' she said.

'Of course. You're my friend.' He thought for a while, and then said, 'The reason I didn't start on an affair with Madeleine was because it wasn't right. Extra-marital affairs are dishonourable.'

After that they continued their walk in companionable silence. But she was thinking about what he had said.

The ridge walk he had brought her on almost described a circle. Before too long they were dropping down the side of another hill, heading for the village again. On the outskirts they found a wooden hut selling mugs of tea, and had one each. Then he noticed her yawning.

'How much sleep did you have last night—this morning?'

'I did all right. I got about three hours in; I've managed with less in the past.'

'Possibly. But you're flagging this time. I was going

to suggest that we have dinner in a pub here, but I think we'd better head for home. We'll find somewhere local to eat.'

Suddenly Kate was weary. She didn't have the strength to object. It was another ten minutes' walk back to the car, and she felt warm and contented after the tea and the walk. She slumped into her seat and felt him leaning over her. 'What're you doing?' she asked drowsily.

'I'm reclining your seat. You'll sleep better that way.'

'I don't need a sleep! It's just being out in the open air that has…'

'Well, just close your eyes for a minute or two.'

'All right,' she said, yawning hugely. 'Steve, this has been a great day. I've really enjoyed myself. We can…'

'The day's not over yet,' he told her.

She awoke when the car stopped and he cut the engine. 'Where are we—what're we doing?' she muttered.

There was a smile in his voice. 'We're back in Kirkhelen. In fact we've just pulled into my surgery. There's couple of papers I'd like to pick up. Would you like to look round, see where I work?'

'Yes, I'd like that. Steve, I didn't intend to sleep all the way. We could have chatted and…'

'It doesn't matter, you needed a rest. Anyway, I quite like looking at you when you're asleep. You look…sweet…vulnerable.'

'Don't even think it,' she told him. 'I'm neither of those.' She felt for the lever, jerked her seat upright.

'If you are still tired I'll run you straight home. Otherwise we could have a meal in a local pub. If you're hungry, that is?'

Firmly, she said, 'Yes, I'm hungry. And, yes, I'd like a pub meal.'

'Good, so would I. Now, there's a light on inside. I wonder who's working late? Let's go and find out.'

She liked the look of the surgery. It was a single-storey, red-brick building, surrounded by lawns and the necessary large car park. By its size she guessed that there would be a central open area. She noted sadly that the windows were covered with ornamental, but very stout grilles. This was necessary in any place where drugs were kept.

Taking a large bunch of keys out, he opened the front door then relocked it behind them. Then he led her down the corridor, pointing out the reception area, the doctors' consulting rooms and the rooms where clinics were held. She was impressed. The decorations, the colour schemes, the layout, all were customer friendly. She wondered how much this was due to Steve's influence.

Finally she followed him into a lighted office. She heard a voice—a very welcoming female voice—say, 'Steve, it's good to see you. What are you doing here?'

He replied, 'Hi, Vanessa, just picking a couple of papers up. More to the point, what are you doing here?'

'You know me. I just can't stop working. We've got the annual returns tomorrow. I want to make sure everything is straight.'

Kate was amused. When Vanessa had spoken to her on the phone she had adopted a much more formal tone. Kate stepped into the room, and Vanessa saw her for the first time. The welcoming smile disappeared at once.

She's older than me, Kate thought cheerfully, possibly older than Steve. Vanessa was very smartly turned out, in grey trousers and a white sweater that was just a bit too tight, and under it a bra that was hitched just a little too high. She was carefully made up; her hair was newly cut. She smiled again—but the smile was different.

'Kate and I have been out for a day on the moors and dropped in to see Amy,' Steve said, apparently quite oblivious of the change in Vanessa's attitude. 'You shouldn't be here on a Sunday night. Anything I could do to help? Anything that can't wait till tomorrow?'

'Well, there are a couple of little points,' Vanessa said, 'if Miss Wilde doesn't mind waiting?'

'No problem,' Kate said sweetly. 'I can always read a magazine.'

'Sorry to be so long,' Steve said when they were back in the car, half an hour later. 'It's not like Vanessa. Those problems could have waited till Monday, but she just had to see to them now.'

'She fancies you and so she distrusts me,' Kate said laconically. 'Anyone can see that.'

Steve glanced at her, confused. 'Not at all. Vanessa is my right hand; I just couldn't run the place without her. She's the best practice manager I've ever come across. She just likes to get things straight.'

'I'm sure she's a magnificent practice manager. But she's still entitled to feelings, isn't she? Has she a current boyfriend? Has she ever been married?'

Steve frowned. 'I don't know about any current boyfriend, but she was certainly married for a while. It was short, very unsatisfactory. The man was a real goon.'

'So no current boyfriend,' Kate mused. 'But she certainly dresses like a woman who is—well, who wants to be interesting.' She thought a minute and then asked, 'Nothing between you, is there?'

'Certainly not,' he said firmly, but Kate caught an edge of uncertainty in his voice.

'Well, has there ever been anything between you?' She wondered to herself why she was pushing this—it wasn't really any of her business—but she just couldn't help it.

'Kate, I don't make a habit of talking about women I've been out with. How would you like it if I talked about you?'

'I'd hate it,' she said robustly. 'But men do talk about women, I know that.'

He sighed. 'I know they do. But I don't. However, I will just say, because I want you to know, that I took Vanessa out to dinner on a couple of occasions. Occasions about a month apart, incidentally. Then I was invited round to her place for an evening meal and I realised that she wanted more from me than I was willing to give. So I told her that this was not good for a professional relationship, and that I hoped we'd always be friends. But that was all. You believe me, don't you?'

She thought a minute. 'Of course I do. You've made it perfectly clear how you see Vanessa. Unfortunately, I don't think she sees you in the same way.' She decided that she'd said enough on the subject. 'Now, where are you taking me?'

'There's a pub quite close called the Waggoner's Arms. They do great evening meals there. I thought we'd have one, and a drink and then I could take a taxi home and you could have an early night.'

'Sounds good,' she said. 'I'd like to spend the entire evening with you, but something is telling me that I'm far more tired than I realised. This past fortnight has been tough!'

He patted her arm—which she liked. 'You'll feel better after an omelette and chips,' he said.

The Waggoner's Arms *was* a good pub. There was no loud music, no fruit machines, no teenagers drinking too much and shouting. But she realised as soon as she entered that she was dead beat. The little sleep she had had in the car had just not been enough. She told him that there was no way she could eat a large meal. Somehow she managed the sandwich and glass of wine that Steve ordered, and in a vague way she enjoyed them. She liked it that he put his arm round her shoulders, and she found her head dropping against his shirt. She didn't talk much.

Then somehow she knew that he was half lifting her, supporting her as she stumbled across the floor and out into the cool evening air. She was in his car for perhaps a minute, and then they were outside her house, and he helped her fumble in her bag for the front door key.

Together they stepped inside the hall, and he kissed her. She was so tired! But she'd liked being kissed, so she kissed him back. For a moment she wondered if…

'Go straight to bed,' his teasing voice said. 'Perhaps we can have another drink tomorrow night. I'll phone you to see.'

'You'll phone me,' she repeated mechanically. 'Goodnight, Steve. I have enjoyed myself.'

She closed the front door and went to the front room window to watch him walk back to his car. He waved. Then she stumbled upstairs and dropped into her bed.

CHAPTER FIVE

IT WAS Monday, the morning after, and she was working on days for a while. Things would change. Accidents in the day tended to be different from accidents at night. Her first case proved this.

'You were doing what, Gerald? I don't believe it!'

Kate had thought she was a cool, experienced A and E nurse, used to the various mad ways that people found to injure themselves. But this was something new. This was a new height—or depth—of stupidity.

Gerald Moore, the young man in front of her, was obviously some kind of professional; she could tell by the slick suit, the crisp shirt. He had been brought in by another man, similarly dressed. Gerald was holding a large dressing to his eye. And, even though he was afraid and in pain, he was still capable of feeling a fool.

'The office has just had this new ceiling fitted—sort of cork tiles with a circular pattern. We thought they looked like dart boards, and one of the lads had a set of darts. So we started throwing them at the ceiling. One of mine stuck in—but when I looked up it fell out again. Right in my eye. Nurse, I'm not going to be blinded am I?' His voice rose in panic.

'We'll do the best we can,' Kate said firmly. 'Now you've had a painkilling injection, I'll fetch the doctor to have a closer look at the eye.'

She wasn't working with Steve this time. But she found Nathan Brand, the young junior registrar who had treated Jo, to be a good, skilful doctor.

Even though Gerald was a grown man, he took comfort in the fact that she was holding his hand. Nathan carefully examined the damaged eye through his ophthalmoscope. Then he said, 'I think we'd better admit you, Mr Moore. We'll get a consultant to have a closer look, but we won't have much idea how permanent the damage is until some of the swelling has subsided.'

'Yes, doctor,' Gerald said.

'So—there's not much difference between English and American A and E?' Nathan was asking the same questions Steve had asked.

'Not a lot,' Kate said cheerfully. 'Both systems work the same way. Nurses work very hard and don't get paid enough. Doctors supervise and get paid too much.'

'Ah. Now I see why you've come back home. But in England both doctors and nurses get paid badly. And to show you how we're all in the same boat, I've decided to share my last chocolate biscuit with you.' From his pocket he took a packet of wafers, snapped three off and threw them across to her.

It had been a hard morning. But now there was time for a rest, and both were sprawled in easy chairs, coffee in hand. The work had brought them together, as it always did. He was a good, methodical worker, and she knew that he found her a very capable nurse. They were a good team. But there wasn't the spark there had been between her and Steve.

'Are you going to stay with us long?' he went on. 'I would have thought that the bright lights of Las Vegas would be calling you. You must have a lot of friends out there—perhaps some particular man?'

Kate tried not to let him see her smile. She knew where his apparently casual questions were leading—he wanted to ask her out. 'Well, I'm not planning on going back quite yet,' she hedged. 'But…'

'Dr Brand, have you got a minute? Staff Nurse Langley would like a word if you're free.' A little auxiliary peered round the edge of the door, and Nathan pushed himself wearily to his feet.

'Staff Nurse Langley's wish is my command,' he said. 'Be right back, Kate.'

Kate nodded and bit into the chocolate biscuit. She had a minute, she'd think about Nathan Brand. It was obvious that Nathan was attracted to her; he'd made it clear in a number of small ways. Soon he'd ask her out; what would she say?

Certainly she enjoyed his company. He was younger than her—just a couple of years—but that didn't matter. She had always said that she would go out with anyone she wanted to, that she was a free spirit. But…what was Steve Russell to her?

He'd only ever kissed her once—actually twice, but she'd been half asleep the last time. She knew he was going to ask her out again. Did she want to go out with him? He'd made it clear that all that he wanted was casual friendship.

In fact he'd phoned her earlier and said that his meeting with Vanessa would be going on far longer than he anticipated. He wouldn't get out for a drink with her as he had hoped.

'You'll be able to share a friendly cup of tea with Vanessa,' Kate had said mischievously.

'Don't start. I came into medicine to deal with ill people, not to fill in forms. Vanessa does a vast amount of the form-filling that I should do. And I'm grateful to her. But I'd much much, much rather be with you.'

'That's nice. I'm going to see Jo, then I think I'll have another early night.'

'Tomorrow looks promising. Can I phone you later?'

'I'll look forward to it.'

So when she came off this shift she would go home and expect a call from Steve. No, she thought. If Nathan asked her, she would not go out with him.

On her lunch break she managed to run upstairs to see Jo. Outside the ward she saw Andrew Kirk, dressed for work in green scrubs. The two of them had met frequently, as the surgeon found time at least once a day to visit her sister. His concern for her was obvious.

'They're talking about Jo being discharged in a couple of days,' he said. 'Are you sure you can cope?'

Kate nodded. This was something she was certain of. 'I can cope. If I can't, then I'll give up work.'

'I hope that won't be necessary. I've heard that apparently you're making a bit of a difference in A and E.' He looked at her thoughtfully. 'Penny—that's my wife—and I are both very fond of Jo. Penny would be very happy for her to come and stay with us. And my two daughters would be delighted.'

Kate shook her head. 'That's very good of you, and I hope you'll all visit, but she's my sister and I'll look after her.'

He grinned. 'Why did I know you'd say that? In some ways, Kate, you're very like Jo. But remember, the offer is there.' He walked off down the corridor.

'So perhaps we'll have you home soon, Jo,' Kate said. 'I've had a word with the ward sister, and she can arrange for you to be brought home when I'll be waiting for you.'

'That'll be nice,' Jo said listlessly. She turned her

head away from her sister, and stared vaguely at the ceiling.

By now, the hurt of the broken leg had largely disappeared. There was some discomfort but the pain had gone. Usually by this time patients were eager to get home, eager to start their life again, irritated by the awkwardness of having to lug a great plaster cast around with them. Not Jo. She had subsided into lethargy; she was interested in nothing.

'You know there's your cloakroom downstairs,' Kate persisted. 'There's a shower, a toilet and a washbasin there. And tonight I'm getting a bed ready to bring down so you can sleep in the living room. I've even got a board to put under the mattress.'

'That'll be fine,' said Jo, totally without interest.

Kate stayed a while longer, talking about unimportant things, mentioning her day's work, trying to get Jo to show some spark of interest. But it was uphill work. Jo didn't contribute anything. Eventually Kate kissed her and went back to work. On the way she stopped for a word with the staff nurse.

'We're worried about her,' the staff nurse said. 'We want her to wake up and fight a bit, get angry at things. But she just lies there. I gather there have been some personal problems?'

'You could say that,' Kate agreed.

'Well, they certainly aren't helping.'

So Kate wasn't in a good mood when she walked back to A and E. However, the minute she got there it was back to work at once.

Nathan was striding down the corridor, moving as fast as was possible without actually running. 'Meet me outside,' he snapped. 'We've got a bad one coming in by ambulance. She's a young girl, a bleeder.'

'Be right there.' Kate scurried to fetch an apron.

The ambulance came up the drive with more than the usual speed, and reversed expertly into the loading bay. The back doors were thrown open, and Kate peered inside.

There was blood everywhere, dripping down the side of the trolley, coating the arm and leg of the paramedic who was leaning over it, pooling on the floor. The driver ran round to the back, and the two paramedics slid the trolley onto the ground.

'Name's Holly Price,' one said efficiently. 'Age sixteen, playing hockey in the park. Holly was running towards the field, tripped over, fell face-first on a broken bottle. Parents have been sent for and are on their way. We just can't stop the bleeding.'

He reached for a sterile bandage pad, ripped it open. Without looking, his partner took it, pressed it against Holly's cheek and dropped the blood-soaked used pad onto the floor.

Swiftly the trolley was wheeled into the first examination room, the little body lifted from the trolley onto the examination couch.

'We need venous access,' Nathan said, 'and quickly.'

Kate was already hooking up the giving set. They would send a sample of Holly's blood to be crossmatched, but for the moment she would be given a unit of O-negative blood. It would do for a while.

Nathan lifted the pad, peered at the gash, then pushed the pad back. 'It's beyond me,' he said honestly. 'We need the maxillo-facial consultant here. I'll get someone to bleep him. Kate, d'you know how to hold this cut closed?'

'I've done it before,' she said. 'I can cope.'

Quite often the easiest way to keep a deep cut from

bleeding was to hold it closed. A pad was never quite as successful. Kate took up a position behind Holly's head, tried to make herself comfortable. This could be a long wait. She felt for the edges of the cut, eased them together with her fingertips. Blood still trickled through, but not as much.

It was a long wait. The man they needed worked at three different hospitals and he had to be fetched. When he finally arrived Kate's arm was stiff and cramped. But the bleeding had nearly stopped.

The consultant examined the wound, nodded at Kate. 'You've done a fine job,' he said. 'I can suture this now.'

She felt she had done a good afternoon's work.

Everything was ready for Jo's arrival home. Kate had moved a small bed into the living room, put the controls of the TV and the music stack nearby, found a bedside table and brought in magazines and a selection of library books. Of course, Jo could move now—slowly and laboriously, but with the help of crutches she could get herself to the cloakroom, or into the kitchen. And if she had her mobile phone with her she could always summon help. Kate looked at her work with pride. Jo was going to be a comfortable invalid.

Kate knew that Steve wouldn't ring in the early evening; he had surgery. So she sat with a cup of tea for a few minutes and watched TV. She'd worked hard; she deserved a rest. English TV was better than American, she decided. Not as much choice—but not as many adverts either.

The phone rang, and her heart leaped. Then she scowled. She knew it would be Steve; why was she so excited? She was cool Kate Wilde. Men interested her but didn't excite her. Not yet, a mean little voice inside her said.

'Kate? How are you? Thoroughly awake yet?'

She had to laugh. 'I guess so. Sorry I fell asleep on you last night, but I really enjoyed the day. Get all your work done with Vanessa?'

'All finished, signed, sealed, sent off by post. Now perhaps I can be a doctor for a week or two. But, before that, can I take you for a real meal tonight? A proper one, where you don't fall asleep on me? It's very threatening to a man's sense of masculinity when he's trying to impress a girl and she promptly goes to sleep.'

'I said I was sorry! Take me out tonight and I promise to be entranced by everything you say. Could we go to the same pub again—the Waggoner's? I don't think I did it justice last time. All I can remember is the very comfortable seats.'

'Henry Saunders, the landlord, is a friend of mine. He'll be upset if all you can remember of his food is that you ate it on a comfortable seat. Shall I pick you up at half past eight?'

'I'm looking forward to it.' She put the phone down with a smile.

Three days previously the first of her packages had come from Las Vegas. She had a wardrobe again. Looking through the clothes hanging in her closet, she decided on a pink silk dress. She had bought it for the hot American evenings, but it would do very well here. She laid it on the bed, found matching dainty underwear, and went for a bath.

It was good to lie there, thick towels warming on the rail, expensive bath oils bubbling gently round her, the smell making her feel cosseted, special. She was really going to enjoy tonight. And then the phone rang again.

She sighed, and reached for a towel. Doesn't this always happen? she asked herself.

On the way to the phone it struck her that perhaps Steve was calling to cancel for some reason, and she moved a little more quickly. But it wasn't Steve.

'I was starting to think you weren't in,' a male voice said, sounding slightly annoyed. She sighed. It was John—phoning from Las Vegas.

Although originally she had refused to give him a number where she could be reached, somehow he had found the name of her hospital, and earlier the week before he had caused havoc by phoning it and insisting that she be found—saying an important call was coming from a surgeon in America. In desperation she had phoned him back and given him her home number.

'I said I'd phone you when I was less busy,' she had pointed out.

John had been unperturbed. 'I only phoned because I was concerned about you,' he had said. 'I'm happier now I know I can get in touch.'

Now he had got her out of the bath; she was dripping wet and unhappy. 'I said I'd phone you this week. What's so important now?'

'You're uptight; I can tell,' that irritatingly calming voice said. 'You're worried about something.'

'I'm uptight because you got me out of the bath, John. Now, just what do you want?'

'Well, I want to know when you're coming back. I managed to stall a committee meeting this morning that was talking about the emergency response team. If you're going to get a place on that programme, then you need to be back here.'

She realised this wasn't the real reason he had rung, but what he said was true. 'I know I should be there.

But I'm not coming back while my sister is ill—if I come back at all.'

'If you come back at all!' John's voice was incredulous. But the minute she had said it, she knew she had said the wrong thing. She also knew that she hadn't thought herself of not going back. The idea had just popped out. Why should she start having doubts now? What had changed? One thing was certain. John hadn't.

'Of course you're coming back,' she heard him say. 'This is just not you. I don't know what's got into you, Kate.'

'Nothing's got into me. I'm just telling you how things are. I'll know better what I'm doing when my sister has fully recovered, but I'm certainly not making any decisions until then. Now I've got to go, John; I've got things to do.'

'Of course,' he said. 'But I'm deeply worried about you, Kate. I'll ring in a couple of days.'

She had calmed down a little by the time Steve came. Her bath water had still been hot, she had enjoyed her soak and then putting on her new silk dress. She was going to enjoy her evening.

When she opened the door to Steve she was even more pleased. His eyes opened in surprise. 'Kate, you look gorgeous,' he gasped.

She knew the outfit suited her. In spite of careful use of sunblock, she was quite tanned. The dress was simply cut, sleeveless and with a moderately deep V-neck. It did a lot for her colouring and her figure.

'I see you've dressed up a little yourself,' she said lightly. 'Come on in.' He was wearing an open-necked white shirt, with a dark suede jacket and darker trousers. And he stood on her doorstep smiling, hands behind his back.

'I've seen hundreds of films about taking American girls out,' he said, 'so I know what to do.' His hand flashed round from behind his back. In it was a bouquet of roses. 'Red roses for romance,' he said.

Kate dropped a little curtsey. 'Oh, gee, what can I say? Come on in and meet Ma and Pop.' Though she thought it herself, it was a pretty good imitation of a mid-west American accent.

She put the flowers in a vase, threw a light cashmere shawl over her shoulders and they walked to his car. It was only a five-minute drive to the Waggoner's Arms. 'I'll probably leave the car here tonight,' he said. 'I feel like just one more than the two drinks I'm entitled to.'

This time, instead of sitting in one of the lounges and asking for a plate of sandwiches, he took her through to the dining room. She loved it—a dark-panelled room with sliding windows opening onto a walled garden. They were expected, and a corner table had been reserved for them.

Kate agreed with him that a bottle of oaked red wine would do very well. She accepted his suggestion that they didn't need a starter, but that the beef Wellington would be an excellent main course. In fact it was a great meal—but she had come out with Steve to talk rather than to eat.

'First of all,' she said, 'just before you came my friend John rang me. I told you about him. He's a doctor at the hospital I worked at. I went out with him a couple of times, and now he thinks he's in love with me. But I don't love him. I'm telling you this because basically I'm an honest person.'

'I'm glad about that, but really I've never doubted it. You've always seemed to me to be a girl who would say...' he pondered a minute '...exactly what she thought, no matter what the consequences.'

She grinned at him. 'Is that a compliment?'

'Well, it makes you exciting to live with. Tell me more about Dr John. Has he any cause to think you're any more to him than you say you are?'

'No,' she said flatly. 'It's just that John's not used to being turned down. He can't understand the idea. Now, that's all I want to say about him—tell me about your day.'

So he did.

After the beef Wellington they didn't feel like a pudding; instead they had the cheeseboard and a glass of port each, followed by a cafetière of coffee and a liqueur. Then they stayed and talked.

'I can't remember when I've enjoyed a meal so much,' she said after a while. 'In fact I can't remember when I've enjoyed anything so much.' She thought a minute, and then went on, 'I guess I've been under a bit of a strain, haven't I? Jo's affected me more than I realised. That walk yesterday did a lot to sort me out, but this is the first really civilised meal I've had since I got home. It's good to be with you, Steve.'

'It's good to be with you too, Kate,' he replied gently, and reached over to stroke the back of her hand.

After a while he glanced at his watch. 'I'm not going to keep you out too late. But I've no intention of driving now. Shall I phone us a taxi, or would you like to walk home? It's only a mile or so; it'd only take a few minutes.'

'I'd really like to walk; it looks to be a wonderful night.'

'Then let's go.'

It was indeed a wonderful night. The heat of the day

had persisted, and they could smell freshly cut grass, the flowerbeds by the side of the road. 'Look,' he said, 'ordered specially to finish off a wonderful evening.'

She glanced upwards. There was the sky, spattered with stars, and a vast full moon.

'I've slept out in the desert quite a lot,' she said. 'The stars there are like nothing I've ever seen.'

'I can well believe it. I've done something similar in the Pyrenees, but I doubt it was anything like the Mojave Desert. Do you miss it all, Kate?'

She considered a minute. 'I thought I would. I intended to go back practically straight away. OK, the weather here is—different, but I'm getting used to it again. And there are a lot of things here making me want to stay. There's Jo, of course, I won't go until she's well, but there's also...' Her voice trailed away.

'What is there also?' His voice teased.

'Lots of other things,' she said firmly. 'And, if you're fishing, I suppose being friends with you is one of those things.'

He walked in silence for a moment, and then said, 'Just friends? Well, that's not exactly a passionate declaration, but I appreciate it, Kate. And I would hate it if you suddenly left.'

He took her hand then. They paced on in silence.

When they got to her home she said, 'Come in and I'll phone for a taxi for you. And would you like another coffee?'

'Not sure about the coffee. But I'd like to come in— and I need a taxi.'

'I'll phone for a taxi at once—and that's all you're invited in for.'

'I might have guessed,' he said mournfully.

They walked into the hall, and as she flicked the

lights on the bulb overhead crackled and died. 'There's something in the atmosphere,' he said.

There was. She could feel it. And although she knew his remark was more than a joke, she decided to say nothing. The dim light at the far end of the hall was just enough to read by, so she took the number of the taxi firm from the card propped up there, and phoned. 'A taxi will be here in fifteen minutes,' she said unsteadily. 'Come into the living room to wait and you can…'

As she turned she bumped into him. The touch was electric. Just that little thing was all that was needed. In the darkened hall his arms went round her, clutched her to him. She didn't resist. She didn't want to resist. He kissed her. Then she realised that she had been wanting this for so long, wanting it and not knowing it. He held her tight to him, his lips demanding, and her mouth opened to him happily. She shared his passion.

Then his grasp slackened, and unconsciously she pulled him closer to her again. His hands caressed her back and shoulders. She could feel his fingertips stroking the sensitive insides of her arms, making shivers run upwards, to her neck and beyond. His lips strayed over her face, as if he had all the time in the world, kissing the corners of her eyes, the smoothness of her forehead, the softness of her cheeks.

All her senses were on fire. She could smell the sharpness of his aftershave, feel the warmth of his body, the slight scratchiness of his beard on her cheek. His heart, her heart, both were beating faster, she didn't know if she was hearing or feeling them. She was aware of his body pressed so close to hers, knew his need for her. She wondered where he was taking her; she didn't care. Her own body seemed liquid with desire. She had never felt like this with any man before.

Something caught the edge of her attention. It was something she should do, and it wasn't going to go away. Then she recognised what it was. The sharp note of a car horn just outside. The taxi had arrived. She tried to shut it out, ignore it. What she was doing was far more important.

But he had heard too. His hold on her relaxed; she heard him sigh. 'That's the taxi. It's early,' he said. 'I should go.'

There was a rising inflection to his voice, as if he was asking her if she thought he might stay. For a moment she was tempted—very tempted. But she had had enough new experiences for one night. Too much, in fact.

'Yes. You'd better go,' she said hoarsely. 'But will you ring me tomorrow? Can you see me tomorrow night?'

His voice too was ragged. 'Nothing will stop me,' he said. 'Nothing. I've got a late surgery, but I'll ring you the minute I finish.'

'You could come here for a late supper. Then we can talk.'

'I'd like that.'

Now their bodies were apart, but they still faced each other, holding hands. In the gloom of the hall she could hardly make out his features, but his expression seemed to be yearning, as if he didn't quite know what to do or say. Neither moved, and then there was the sound of the taxi horn again.

'You'd better go,' she said. 'You'll be getting me a bad name with the neighbours.' It seemed such a pro-

MILLS & BOON®

An Important Message from
The Editors of Mills & Boon®

Dear Reader,

Because you've chosen to read one of
our romance novels, we'd like to say
"thank you"!

And, as a **special way** to thank you,
we've selected <u>four more</u> of the
<u>books</u> you love so much **and** a welcome
gift to send you absolutely <u>FREE!</u>

Please enjoy them with our
compliments...

Tessa Shapcott

Editor, Mills & Boon

P.S. And because we value our
customers we've attached
something extra inside...

EDITOR'S
"THANK
YOU"
SEAL

PEEL OFF AND PLACE INSIDE

saic thing to say, and it jarred with the turbulence of emotions she was feeling.

Reluctantly, he turned, opened the door, then bent for one last kiss. 'Goodnight, darling,' he said, and went.

Through a gap in the living room curtains she watched the taxi drive away. Then, moving like a robot, she went upstairs to undress, showered and wrapped a towel round herself. She came down to the kitchen, made herself a mug of cocoa and went back to her bedroom. She didn't switch on the light.

The night was still warm. She opened the curtains and the window, and let the soft night air play over her naked, still damp body. It felt so good. For a while she was happy just to stand there, to feel rather than think. But then she sighed. The last hour *had* happened. She would have to think about it. She would have to make decisions.

She had known that Steve would kiss her sooner or later. In fact, he had already done so. But this last kiss had been the urgent kiss of a lover. And she had responded. Whatever there had been between her and Steve before had now turned into something far, far different.

She had never felt like this before. She had never known this electric response, when her entire body thrilled to a man's. Apprehension warred with excitement. This was something she couldn't give up.

Always, she had been in control of her emotions, her feelings. Perhaps it was because of the way she had been brought up, but she had learned never to reveal too much of herself to anyone—except Jo, of course. And now she knew she was not in control. Her feelings were running riot. She wasn't sure that she liked it.

Of course she liked it! She remembered the sheer joy of being in his arms. But she had packed so much emotion into the last few days. Perhaps she was still tired—Steve had warned her of that. Yes, that was it. She was tired. Soon she would be back to normal. She'd be in control—she'd be her old tough self. Then she could sort out what she was really thinking, and what she would have to do.

She realised also that there was something else she perhaps ought to worry about. Steve had loved her twin sister. Was he now falling for her, Kate Wilde, or just for someone who reminded him of a lost love? He had told her that he had no difficulty in separating his feelings for the two. Kate pondered for a minute, then decided he was telling the truth. His feelings were for her now.

She rolled onto her bed, pulled a sheet over her still damp body. Surprisingly, within seconds she was asleep.

Nearly the end of the afternoon shift. Carefully, Kate pressed butterfly stitches onto the arm of an eight-year-old who had cut himself in the playground. He sat stolidly on the knee of Miss Frith, his schoolteacher, who had confessed quietly to not really liking blood, and who had looked well away when Kate irrigated the wound.

What would she have done if she'd been faced with yesterday's victim, Holly Price? Kate wondered to herself. This morning she had phoned to ask about the girl. The verdict was cautiously optimistic. Holly had spent a reasonable night and was now comfortable. It was too early to decide about her face—but she might need plastic surgery. For a moment Kate wondered about the kind of person who would throw a broken bottle into the grass round a playing field—and then decided she had better things to think about.

The last stitch was pressed into place. 'All done, Kevin,' Kate said. 'You've been a brave boy; here's a sweet and a badge for you.'

'Thank you, miss,' said Kevin. Still perfectly calm, he put the sweet in his mouth and the badge on the front of his sweater. Kate wished all her patients were like Kevin.

'There's no need for Kevin to come back to us,' Kate said to Miss Frith. 'He can go to his own GP and have another dressing put on. D'you know where his mother is?'

'We phoned her but she was out,' Miss Frith said. 'Perhaps she was shopping or something. And I know his father is away. I'll take Kevin back to school.'

'Well, don't let him go back in the playground. He should rest somewhere quiet and perhaps not come into school tomorrow. All right, Kevin?'

'I can sit in the activity centre,' said Kevin, still stolid.

'We'll have to fill in an accident form now,' Miss Frith said gloomily. 'Then it'll have to be brought up in the safety committee meeting, and afterwards reported to the governors.'

'Safety *is* very important,' Kate said.

'I know it is. But now there are reports, meetings, sub-committees, recommendations, and then more meetings. They all take time. What happened to teaching?'

Kate managed not to let Miss Frith see her smiling, but she thought she could sympathise with the woman. She walked with the couple to the front door.

'Enjoying work with us, Nurse Wilde? Are our primitive methods as good as those in America?'

Kate looked up, and there was Nursing Manager Margaret Welsh. Kate hadn't seen much of her while she'd been working the night shift, but Nathan had told her that the nursing manager had asked for detailed reports on her work. 'I told her that you were exceedingly competent and also very attractive,' he had said. 'But the second bit wasn't what Margaret wanted to hear.' Kate had sighed at that.

Now she decided she didn't mind Margaret Welsh asking for reports on her; the woman was entitled to try to run a good department. And she decided also—just for once—to overlook the woman's unpleasant remarks about American hospitals.

'Injured people are injured people anywhere,' she said cheerfully. 'And bandages are bandages.'

'A very healthy attitude.' Margaret smiled a thin smile. 'I'm glad we were able to offer you work on the Bank. Though I don't know if we'll be able to find you work for much longer.'

This surprised Kate. From what she could see, there was a desperate need for her and this need would continue. But Margaret went on, 'And I hope you're not expecting a permanent job. There's absolutely no chance of that.'

Kate wasn't going to confide any possible change in her plans to this woman. And she certainly couldn't be bothered to have an argument with her. So she said, 'I wouldn't apply if there was a full-time job. I expect to be off again—when my sister is fully better.'

The moment she said this she realised it was not true. A few weeks ago it might have been true. But now...

However, it was obviously the right thing to say.

Margaret smiled and relaxed a little. 'I gather you've had to work right through the afternoon without a break. Come to my room; we can have a drink together.'

'All right,' said Kate, rather surprised at this. She followed the woman into her tiny office and accepted a mug of weak coffee. Margaret sat opposite her.

'I gather you were out with Dr Russell last night,' she said carelessly. 'You had a nice meal in the Waggoner's, didn't you?'

'How did you know we were there?' Kate asked cautiously.

Margaret shrugged. 'Friends of mine were having a meal there; we all go from time to time. Dr Russell takes Vanessa there quite often. I gather you've met my daughter?'

'Yes, I have. You're a lot like her.'

Margaret smiled a little more. 'Thank you, that's nice to know.'

In fact Kate had been thinking of the thin lips and the generally unpleasant attitude, but she decided not to mention this.

'It was Vanessa who gave up quite a lot of her time to help with your sister's...troubles,' Margaret went on, watching Kate closely.

By now Kate was wary. 'I—we—were very grateful,' she said. 'Perhaps I'll be able to do something like that for her one day.' So far, so calm. She was holding onto her temper.

Margaret gave a little tinkling laugh. 'Oh, I doubt that will be necessary. You know, our family and Dr Russell's family have known each other for years. In fact Stephen and Vanessa were almost brought up together—they were childhood sweethearts. He was so sad when Vanessa went off and married that evil man—

but Stephen gave her a job and they're very good friends now.'

Suddenly Kate realised what was happening. She was being warned off! Margaret was telling her that Stephen was Vanessa's, and she was not to poach! Kate wasn't sure whether to be angry or to be amused. Certainly she knew the best thing to do would be to keep quiet, to mollify Margaret, to let her think that she was no threat to the precious Vanessa. After all, the woman was almost her employer.

But life was too short for that kind of behaviour. She was just not having it.

She smiled sweetly, and said, 'I like Stephen a lot myself, and I'm hoping to see a lot more of him. You know he took me out yesterday? I'd like to respond in some way. Could you recommend a restaurant where we could have dinner—somewhere cosy and intimate? Of course, I could always invite him to dinner at home. He might like to try American cooking—something a bit different?'

She looked eagerly at the speechless Margaret. Then she wondered if perhaps she had gone a little too far. Margaret looked as if she had bitten something sour; she was not amused. Her face was white and there was a pinched look to her lips.

Before Margaret could reply, there was a knock on the door and a nurse looked in. 'Kate, you've got a visitor. You'd better come.'

Kate frowned, said 'Excuse me' to Margaret, and hurried out.

'He's knock-out gorgeous,' the nurse whispered as Kate passed her.

Followed by Margaret, Kate walked rapidly down the corridor. She walked into the reception area. It seemed as if everyone in A and E was there. There were doctors, nurses, porters, auxiliaries, even some patients. In the middle of the floor was a pile of expensive luggage. And in front of the luggage, tall, good-looking, dressed in a beautifully cut light grey suit, was John Bellis.

What was he doing here? He should be in Las Vegas! She looked at him, open-mouthed, horror-struck.

Before she could get over her bewilderment, John strode forward, grabbed her and kissed her enthusiastically, to the delight of everyone but her.

'So good to see you, kid,' John said. 'You don't know how much I've missed you.'

She managed to wriggle free from his grip. But Margaret had seen her advantage, had come to stand by her side. 'Aren't you going to introduce us, Kate?' She smiled.

Unable to find words for once in her life, Kate stuttered and stammered.

John found words for her. 'Hi,' he said, offering his hand to Margaret. 'I am Dr John Bellis and I've come to find my fiancée Kate, here, and take her back to America with me.'

'It's so good to hear that,' cooed Margaret. 'I'm sure the news will fascinate everyone.'

CHAPTER SIX

FORTUNATELY it was nearly the end of her shift. 'I'm still working,' she said to John. 'Stay there until I come to get you. I'll be about ten minutes.'

'Take all the time you like, sweetheart,' John said urbanely. 'I'll just sit here and drink coffee.'

'And don't call me… Oh, why do I bother?'

There was a definite protocol at the end of the shift. She made sure all her notes and observations were filed in the correct place, then walked along for hand-over to make sure that the relieving nurse knew what problems they had.

When she had finished she wondered what to do. She had intended to call on Jo for a while—but no way would she take John up to see her sister. For a moment she even considered just disappearing through a back exit, but she knew it would do no good. John was dogged; he would find her and cause no end of trouble while he was looking. She went back to Reception.

There were always taxis outside the A and E Department. Kate beckoned one, told John to load his baggage and climbed in with him. It seemed as if half the hospital came out to watch them drive away.

'What's this nonsense about you being my fiancé? Don't you know what hospitals are? It'll be all over the place in five minutes.'

John looked hurt. 'Well, we are good friends, and since you've been away I've had time to think. I'm sure

104

you have too. I think that we've got something going, Kate, and we've both got to work at it.'

It was so frustrating. 'We've talked about this before. Didn't I make myself clear? I said we were friends, no more.'

'That was then. I was sure you were getting to feel the same way as I do. After talking to you yesterday I realised you were really upset. I had a little time owing, so I came over at once. To help you. Aren't you pleased to see me?'

Not for the first time, she wondered which planet John had arrived from. 'Well, it's nice that you can think of me. But honestly, John, there's no future for us.'

For the first time John looked a little confused, a little crestfallen. 'I didn't think you'd act this way,' he said.

Kate sighed. 'Well, I *am* acting this way. Now, where are you going to stay?'

'Can't I stay with you? I know you've got a house, and I thought…'

'You're not staying in the house. Not a chance! I'll find you a good hotel.' She leaned forward and directed the taxi driver to the Royal Lancaster. She knew it was the best—and most expensive—hotel in Kirkhelen. But John was a surgeon; he could easily afford it. And he'd be comfortable there.

In fact there was a suite vacant, and John thought it would be fine. The plumbing was up to standard, there was a good view of the church from the front window, and there was twenty-four-hour room service.

'We are a little bit civilised in this country,' she told him.

'It's just that you hear such stories,' John said. 'And I take it you're not going to stay here with me?'

This was said with a definite hopeless tone. Perhaps at last he was getting the message. 'No, I'm not staying here with you. In fact my sister will be coming home from hospital in the next couple of days; I'll be spending all my spare time with her. It's just not convenient for you to come now, John, though I do appreciate the thought.'

'Well, will you at least have dinner with me this evening? After all, I've flown all this way to see you.'

Of course this was true. She'd have to give way on something. 'All right,' she said, 'I'll meet you downstairs in the cocktail bar at eight.'

She nearly changed her mind when she saw the delighted expression on his face, but she didn't. Why, oh, why did John have to turn up now?

It was on her way back to hospital by taxi to see Jo that she remembered that she had arranged to see Steve that evening. He was going to phone her and then he was coming over. This was too bad! She'd have to phone Steve and explain as best she could—and she couldn't really explain things to herself.

Once in the hospital, she made for the battery of phones in the lobby and dialled Steve's surgery. Worst of luck, she got through to Vanessa.

'I'm so sorry,' Vanessa said, sounding polite but anything but sorry. 'I can't possibly connect you to Dr Russell. He's seeing patients now, and we have strict instructions not to put through any personal calls whatsoever.'

'Not even in emergencies?' Kate asked, grinding her teeth.

'I'm afraid not. But if it's a medical emergency you should phone the hosp…'

'It's not a medical emergency. Dr Russell was going to come round for supper, but I've had an unexpected guest turn up and…'

'Your fiancé!' Vanessa said cheerfully, obviously enjoying the situation. 'My mother told me about him coming. It must be really exciting for you.'

'He's not my fiancé! But I have to have dinner with him tonight, at the Royal Lancaster, and I wanted to explain…' Suddenly she had an idea. 'Ask Steve to call me, will you? As soon as he gets out of surgery. I don't know where I'll be but he can reach me on my sister's mobile.' She scrabbled in her bag for the number. 'I don't usually carry it, but I will tonight.' Kate read out the number.

'I'll pass on the message, Miss Wilde,' said Vanessa. 'Now you must excuse me. There's another call coming in, and it could be someone needing a doctor urgently.'

'It could indeed,' Kate agreed, and rang off. For a moment she stood, oblivious of the crowds passing her. Nearly lost my temper there, she thought. I'm going to have to watch Vanessa.

Jo was as quiet as ever. Kate borrowed her mobile phone—it was by the bedside, and Jo had been telling her to take it for days. Then she told Jo about John turning up—making light of her irritation, though. For once, Jo smiled; she was amused. Then Kate caught herself. She didn't want Jo to know exactly how fond she was getting of Steve. Not that she was at all ashamed of it. But Jo had suffered enough because of the Russells.

She went home, cleaned up for a while, and then showered and changed into the same pink dress that she had worn yesterday. She knew she looked well in it—but there was not the same anticipation as there had been when she went out with Steve.

All the time she kept Jo's mobile phone with her. She had made sure it was charged—once before she had suffered because her battery was low. She thought— well, she wondered and hoped—that perhaps Steve might get the message early, and call her before she went out. She wanted to explain things to him quietly, when there was no one around. But then she decided that there was no chance of Vanessa passing on the message till the last possible minute. Still, she felt more and more disappointed as the minutes ticked by.

At half past seven she phoned for a taxi to take her to the Royal Lancaster. She decided to ask Jo next day if she could start using her car; she'd need it in the future to ferry her sister round the town.

When she first got into the taxi, the mobile firmly gripped in her hand, she felt angry. She should be going out with Steve, not John. But then she calmed a little. She supposed it was something of a tribute to have a man fly over from America just to see her. She'd just have to explain—again—that they were friends but nothing more.

It was also rather pleasant to walk into the Royal Lancaster. She knew she looked well, and she was aware of the discreetly turned heads, the odd quiet comment. It was nice to be admired!

John was waiting at the bar in the cocktail lounge, wearing a suit so pale as to be almost white. As ever, he was charming some young lady, this time a young waitress who was obviously impressed. As Kate drew nearer she could hear that oh, so sincere voice. 'As a medical doctor, I know what can happen. Alcohol is a poison! There are fruit drinks that are...'

'In that case you can poison me,' Kate interrupted him. 'I'd like a glass of dry red wine, please.'

She felt a bit sorry for the waitress as John promptly transferred his attentions to her. 'Kate! My God, you look stunning! And that dress is to die for!'

He moved round the table towards her. Kate, feeling that she had been kissed quite enough by him for one day, nimbly put a chair in between them. 'Sit down, John. And, as I said, I'll have a glass of dry red wine, please.'

Good-natured as ever, John gave up his pursuit of her and held out the chair for her before giving the order to the waitress. 'I've got a table reserved next door for later,' he said as he settled himself. 'I'm being made very comfortable here, but it's not Vegas, is it?'

'No, it isn't Vegas,' she said. 'But this hotel was thriving before the Pilgrim Fathers landed in Virginia.'

'Ah,' said John. 'Well, yes, that is something.'

'Anyway, what's with this alcohol poisoning idea? You were happy to drink wine the last time I saw you.'

It turned out that John had been for a fitness assessment. The trainer had told him to eat less, lose weight, exercise more and stop drinking.

'Health Fascist,' Kate said breezily. 'Now, I for one am ravenous. Can we go straight into the dining room?'

'Just as you wish,' said John urbanely.

The dining room was very pleasant, she had to admit. However, she would have preferred the Waggoner's. The meal too was excellent. John stuck to a steamed fruit and vegetable diet, but she had worked hard that day and felt she was entitled to more wine and to something fried. So she enjoyed her rare steak.

She decided to eat, before trying to have an honest conversation with John. Perhaps she wasn't being entirely fair to him. It was certainly good of him to come out here out of concern for her—or was it concern for him? Whatever it was, he had to be put right about their relationship—though she felt she had been clear enough so far. And why hadn't her mobile rung yet? It was now well past eight o'clock. Where was Steve?

Feeling reasonably at peace with the world after the meal, she walked with John into the lounge for coffee. It was a big room in the English country club style. There were lots of leather chairs, panelled walls, large numbers of brasses. She felt as if she was in a Christmas card. A few people were sitting there in expensive suits, and at the far end was a bar.

They sat in an alcove, and a large silver coffee pot was carried in on an even larger silver tray. Two cups were poured—no sugar for John—and she decided that this was the time to try to explain—again. 'Now, look, John,' she started, 'I like you a lot, but...'

Their alcove faced down the room. At the far end, the door opened—and in came Vanessa. She was looking quite smart, Kate had to admit. She was wearing the classical little black dress, with black tights and pumps, and silver accessories. She was well made-up and her hair was just right. Vanessa had dressed to impress, and Kate marvelled that she had managed to do so, so quickly.

Walking in behind her, in a dark suit, was Steve.

With slightly more force than was necessary, Kate put her cup down in her saucer. Steve hadn't phoned her. She had to wonder exactly what message Vanessa had given him—she suspected not the complete one.

Vanessa had glanced round the room. Kate was sure she had seen her, but Vanessa gave no sign. Instead she

turned to Steve and spoke to him in a laughing voice,
so he had to look at her.

'Here's some friends of mine,' Kate said rapidly to
John. 'Steve's a doctor; you'll like him.' Then she was
on her feet, walking across the room, speaking in a
slightly louder voice than was really necessary.

'Steve—and Vanessa. Good of you to bring her,
Steve. We're over here, plenty of room for four. Come
and meet John.'

'Well, really,' said Vanessa, 'he didn't exactly bring
me. I brought…'

Kate looked at Steve, whose face remained inscru-
table. But something told her that he knew exactly what
was happening. 'You would like to join us, wouldn't
you, Steve?' she asked.

'Of course,' said Steve urbanely, 'if you're sure we're
not intruding. I'd love to meet your friend. Wouldn't
you, Vanessa?'

'I'd love to meet him,' Vanessa muttered.

John's manners were always impeccable. He stood as
they approached, arranged the seating, shook hands and,
as the perfect host, insisted on ordering the drinks.
There was more waiting, more shuffling around until
the waitress returned, and then everyone had a drink in
their hand and it was time to talk.

'Rather a pointed question when you've just arrived,'
Steve said to John, 'but are you staying here long?'

John shook his head. 'Not at all. I came over to try
to persuade Kate to come back quickly. There's a good
job waiting for her—prospects are excellent. But she
has to get in there and pitch for it.'

Kate saw Vanessa look a lot brighter. 'And I've just
told John I can't go and pitch, because I'm not coming

back in the foreseeable future,' she said cheerfully. 'In fact I might well decide to stay here for good.'

Judging by their expressions, this was not good news, neither for Vanessa nor John. But the corners of Steve's mouth twitched. Obviously he found something amusing about this. 'You can't even think of going back until Jo's a lot better,' he said. 'And after that, who knows what life might have in store for you?'

Is he trying to tell me something? she thought.

After that the conversation became more general. There was no attempt to explain why Vanessa was there with Steve, and Kate decided not to ask about the message she had left. Things were going well enough.

Surprisingly—or perhaps not—Steve and John got on quite well and found a lot to talk about. To Vanessa's dismay Steve offered John the chance to come and look round his surgery; John accepted eagerly. For a while it looked as if the two men were going to talk between themselves, leaving the women to talk about to each other. But neither Kate nor Vanessa was going to have that. The conversation became more general, about the difference between American and British medicine.

It was still quite early when Kate saw John trying to stifle a yawn, and realised he hadn't been to bed for over twenty hours. 'You're jet-lagged,' she said. 'You need to get upstairs to bed. And I could do with an early night myself. Vanessa, Steve, I think you'd better excuse us.'

'Not at all,' Steve said politely. 'In fact I'm ready to go myself. How about you, Vanessa?'

'Well...' Vanessa said sulkily, then decided not to push her luck. 'I suppose I'm ready to go too.'

'Can we offer you a lift home?' Steve then asked

Kate, and Kate had difficulty not laughing as she saw Vanessa's face look even more gloomy.

'I'd love a lift if it's not out of your way,' she said.

Then she held out her hand to John. 'Goodnight, John. I'm working tomorrow, but I'll give you a ring here in the evening and we'll think about things you can do while you're here.'

'Things I can do with you?' he asked hopefully.

'Not for much of the time. You understand my sister's coming out of hospital either tomorrow or the day after, and I'll have to look after her.'

'Of course.' There was more handshaking and Steve led his two ladies into the car park.

Vanessa very pointedly took the front seat. Well, Kate thought, she had come in it. The atmosphere in the car was not conducive to conversation, especially when Vanessa discovered it was more convenient for Steve to drop her off before Kate. 'But I thought you might come in for coffee,' she said petulantly.

'We can have coffee in the surgery tomorrow,' Steve said, and the touch of irony in his voice suggested that Vanessa had better say nothing more.

There was a frozen, 'Goodnight, Miss Wilde,' as Steve held the door for her to climb out of the car. Then Kate scurried out of the back and jumped into the front seat. Vanessa saw this, but said nothing.

As the car moved away, Kate said, 'D'you think we could keep quiet just for five minutes? I feel as if I've been over a verbal assault course.'

'Of course,' Steve said amiably. 'Pick a tape if you wish.' So they listened to Elton John as he drove to Kate's home.

'Will you come in for a coffee with me?' she asked

as they reached her front door. 'If you're tired you don't have to, but…'

'You promised me an evening out with you,' he said gently. 'I mean just you. And I'm still looking forward to it. Yes, I'd love to have a coffee.'

They walked into her living room; she switched on a couple of low lights. 'Now you pick the music while I make the coffee,' she said, 'and then we can have a talk.'

When she came back, he had taken off his coat and tie and was sitting on the couch with his shirt unbuttoned, listening to *Songs for Swinging Lovers* by Sinatra. 'You're an old romantic,' she said.

'Nothing like a touch of mood music.'

She pulled the low table near to the couch, placed the tray on it and then sat with her knees drawn up, looking at him. 'I told you before,' she said, 'I want things between us out in the open. I don't like it when people try to manipulate me, or interfere with me. I make my own decisions about serious things. I didn't know John was coming, and I don't want him here. But since he is here, and he's a friend, I shall try to look after him. A bit. But there was never anything serious between us. It's just that I can't persuade him of it.'

'He seems a nice chap,' Steve said cheerfully. 'I like his taste in women—and in clothes, for that matter.'

'Be serious! I know you don't like talking about ex-girlfriends, but I have no such problems talking about ex-boyfriends. I…'

'It doesn't matter, Kate. I understand John, and I sympathise with him a little bit. I think you're worth fighting for.'

She felt more at ease now. 'I'm glad we've got that

sorted. Just so long as you know that there's nothing between us, and that I'm completely fancy-free.'

'Completely fancy-free? Just when I was hoping you might have a soft spot for me.'

'Hmm. Well perhaps I have a soft spot for you. A small one, but it might grow. Incidentally, what was the message you got from Vanessa?'

He laughed gently. 'You mustn't think I'm completely dim, Kate. Now you've made me think about it, I know what she's up to. The message was changed—quite subtly. In fact she invited me to the Royal Lancaster. I presume that she thought that if I saw you with a boyfriend I'd want nothing more to do with you.'

He sighed. 'Until now I've thought this—infatuation—was no great problem. But it's getting to be one. I'll have to talk to her. I don't want to lose her; she's a very good practice manager.'

'She wants to manage you as well as the practice,' Kate said darkly, 'and I'm not sure I trust her mother either.'

This time he laughed. 'I'm my own man,' he said. 'I decide what I want to do. Now, tell me about Jo.'

Kate looked worried. 'The broken leg is doing well—she'll be home in a day or so, and then it'll be one long programme of physiotherapy and recuperation. But she doesn't seem to care either way. She's still very low after the wedding was called off. I try to cheer her up—but it does no good.'

'Will she talk about Harry?'

'No. If I even hint about him she just clams up. Perhaps if she *did* talk…'

'Just wait till she's ready. Grief works in strange ways. The best thing you can do is love her and be there for her.'

'She's my twin sister. I know that.'

There was silence for a moment—a friendly, contemplative silence. Then he reached out across the couch and put his arm round her, pulled her closer to him and kissed her. 'Sometimes,' he said, 'I think we spend too much time talking and not enough doing.'

It felt good to lie there, being kissed by him. She felt no pressure, just an easy enjoyment of his and her body. They seemed to fit so well together—each knew what would give pleasure to the other.

After a while—when she was ready—his hand strayed to the back of her neck. She felt his fingers undo the button at the top of her dress and then slowly draw down the zip.

'Those are the deft hands of a doctor,' she whispered.

Now his hands were on the sides of her face, and his kiss grew more intense. Then she felt him gently take her dress and ease it off her shoulders. She couldn't stop him. With a sudden thrill she realised she didn't want to stop him. Whatever he wanted to do, she wanted him to do. Never before had she felt this way with a man.

There was a rush of excitement, bodily excitement. She knew her pulse was racing, could feel her breathing becoming deeper, her skin warming, sensitising under his touch. She knew that he felt the same way. In the dim light she could see his passion-darkened eyes, his urgency. This man struck to her very soul.

The front of her pink dress lowered. She moved her shoulders and it fell to her lap. With a finger he traced the curve of her breast, to the silk lace of her half-cup bra. Her breath raced faster than ever; she could feel her nipples tauten with anticipation. A hand felt behind her, and a second later the bra was loosened and then fell.

Gently, he pressed her backwards on the couch. There was nothing she could do. Her body felt liquid with desire. Then he leaned over her and in turn took each breast into his mouth. She cried aloud with the excitement of it. Never before had she felt like this. She threw her arms round him, pulled his head away and down onto her own eager lips. She thrust her hands inside his opened shirt, felt the throbbing of his heart— as fast as her own. The crispness of the hair on his chest excited her passion, made it stronger.

She knew she wanted just to be with this man, wanted to be with him entirely—to give him everything.

Everything?

She had always been level-headed; the life she had led had taught her to be cautious. Gently, sadly, she eased him away. He was responsive to her mood. He knew something was wrong and he let her do so.

'Kate…what's the matter. I don't understand…?' His voice was hoarse, uncomprehending.

'Drink your coffee,' she said, and then realised this wasn't enough. She had to tell the full truth. 'Steve, we were getting carried away there. You know where we were going. Well, before …or if… I want to think about it. I'm not all that tough. I'm a nervous girl. Sometimes, I…' She looked at him anxiously. 'Steve, you don't think that I'm a tease, do you? I don't want you to think that. I just need…a little more time.' Then she managed to struggle upright.

Somehow, he managed to laugh, and she knew what an effort it had cost him. He reached for his coffee. His hand must have been trembling; the cup rattled in the saucer. 'Kate, I think you're marvellous, and I think you're honest. No, I don't think you're a tease.'

Now she was regretting stopping him. She reached

for her coffee, took a great swallow. 'We're still friends?' she asked plaintively.

He put his arms round her shoulders, then, to her amazement, reached down and pulled up the top of her dress. 'We're much more than friends,' he said.

CHAPTER SEVEN

NEXT morning Kate went to hospital early, intending to see her sister before starting at A and E. The day was going to be fine, perhaps hot later. But now there was dew on the grass, and as she walked across the little front lawn she left footprints behind. For a moment she contrasted this delicate weather with the brassy heat she knew there would be in Las Vegas. At the moment, she thought she preferred this.

Perhaps Jo was a little better. Or perhaps it was Kate's own good mood that was infectious. Whatever, her sister seemed to be almost looking forward to getting home. 'I'm fed up with being in hospital,' she grumbled. This was good. So far she hadn't cared where she was.

Kate was in a good mood because Steve had to visit the hospital later, and before they'd parted last night they had arranged to meet in the canteen for lunch. It would only be for half an hour—but she was looking forward to it.

As usual, she started work with Nathan. Their first patient was Jenny Fisk—a sullen seventeen-year-old with rings through her nose, her eyebrow and her lip. 'I'm pregnant,' she announced belligerently, 'and I think I'm losing it.'

'Have you taken anything?' Nathan asked gently. 'Done anything to yourself?'

'I didn't try to get rid of it; it just happened. Ow!' Jenny clutched her abdomen and bent over.

'Let's get you undressed, Jenny,' Kate said, 'then Doctor can examine you.'

It turned out that this was the first time Jenny had been to see a doctor. Jenny was convinced that the family GP would tell her mother what had happened.

'Me and Will, we only done it once,' she said, 'and he didn't use anything because he's too stupid. Then my periods got ever so small, and my belly started swelling. And it hurts.'

Kate looked at Nathan, who had just reappeared. 'How long ago was this, Jenny?' she asked.

'About three months.' Jenny's face contorted as another pang shook her.

'Let's examine you, shall we?' Nathan asked. 'Nurse, can you ask for the ultrasound?'

'Yes, Doctor.' This was an unconfirmed pregnancy; there could be a variety of reasons for Jenny's condition. If it was a pregnancy it could be ectopic—not in the uterus. Or it could even be some kind of tumour. Already, Kate was doubting that Jenny was having a baby.

Shortly afterwards the technician wheeled the ultrasound machine in. Kate smeared the gel over Jenny's abdomen and then Nathan started to sweep the probe across it. 'Can you see the baby?' asked Jenny. 'Can I see it now?' Kate noted that suddenly Jenny seemed almost eager.

'I'm afraid there's no baby to see, Jenny.'

Kate covered Jenny up and the technician took away his machine. Then Nathan said, 'You never were pregnant Jenny. I think you've got an ovarian cyst. We'll have to admit you, of course, and I'm afraid you'll have to have an operation. Now, how can we get in touch with your mother? The sooner she knows, the better.'

'So, I'm not having a baby?'

'I'm afraid not, Jenny.'

Jenny burst into tears. 'But I wanted it really,' she said.

Nathan looked across at Kate and shrugged.

Kate was entitled to a lunch break, and could take it more or less when she wanted. Of course, no nurse in A and E would leave if there was any kind of emergency—but this morning, after Jenny, things seemed to be unusually quiet. So much so that Margaret Welsh noticed that Kate had spent rather a long time just drinking coffee, and found her another job.

'The hospital auditors need to know exactly what stores we have,' she said with a thin smile. She handed Kate a folder of papers and led her to the largest storeroom. 'Count everything and enter how many we have in the appropriate column on one of these sheets. There are usually stock numbers on items, that should make things easier. Please be careful. This is an important and an urgent job.'

Kate looked at the filled shelves and groaned to herself. This could take for ever. 'Isn't this a ward clerk's job?' she asked tentatively.

'Our ward clerk is busy. You aren't.'

This was true. Kate took the folder and started work.

Ten minutes before she was due to meet Steve, she counted the final packet of bandages and decided to stop. She'd finish the stock-taking in the afternoon—unless a real nurse's job came along. She hoped it would. She opened the stockroom door—and there was Margaret Welsh.

'Where are you going, Nurse Wilde?'

Kate looked at her in surprise. 'I'm going for lunch. I'll finish the job this afternoon.'

'I told you, this task is urgent. You can go for a break when you've finished.'

'I've arranged to meet someone,' Kate said quietly. Then she saw that, just for a moment, an expression of triumph had appeared on Margaret's face. 'But you already knew that, didn't you?' Kate asked, and slowly took off her apron. 'Well, I'm going for my break now. As you know, I would happily stay for any emergency, but I don't think counting syringes is an emergency. I'll be back at the proper time.'

'If you leave now don't expect any more work!'

Kate could have laughed. The days when she'd stand for being bullied were long since gone. 'If I don't get more work, then I'll make an official complaint against you. I've joined the union. Just think what they'd make of this at a tribunal meeting. I'd happily tell them the personal reasons behind your victimisation.'

She saw Margaret's white face turn mottled, and realised she had really frightened the woman.

'Look,' she said patiently, 'I think you're a good boss; I can work under you quite happily. Just don't threaten me. It's not my fault if your plans for your daughter don't work out. Now, is it all right if I go now?'

There was no reply. She took it that this meant assent.

When she entered the canteen she looked round and Steve stood and waved her over. Her heart gave a little bounce. She had last seen him only a few hours before, but still the sight of him excited her. He was dressed in a doctor's dark suit, but with a cheerful floral tie, and she was so happy to see him.

'Since you weren't here I queued up and bought you

a salad, a pot of tea and a strawberry cream tart,' he said. 'And here's a chair, specially reserved.'

She sat. 'That's good of you. How did you know that a strawberry tart was the way to my heart?'

'Hmm. How did I know you were a poet? Well—I was wondering if after last night you might be having second thoughts. If you were I was going to console myself with confectionery.'

'And I was wondering if you might not be coming,' she replied. 'What I did was a bit—well, a lot thought-less. But if it's any consolation, it hurt me as much as it hurt you.'

'I'm sure it did,' he said, and she blushed slightly.

'John Bellis phoned me this morning,' he said. 'We had a chat and I've arranged for him to look round my surgery.'

'You pick a strange way to make new friends,' she said with a grin.

'I do genuinely like the man. Look, Kate, you've made the situation between you and him very clear, and I understand. But the man's flown all the way from America, apparently thinking he was going to help you. What I'm saying is, don't freeze him out on my ac-count. Have dinner with him again, see something of him. I don't mind and I won't be jealous.'

'Not even a little bit?'

He looked hunted. 'Kate, it's very hard, but I'm try-ing to do the graceful thing. Give me a bit of credit for acting properly. Anyway, he said he was thinking of going down to London for a couple of days.'

'Ah,' she said. 'So your noble offer to give me up wasn't as noble as I thought. Good. Now, if he's going to London, then I'll arrange to show him a bit of the local scenery first.'

They both ate salad for a while, apparently contented with the way their meeting was going.

After a while he said, 'Look around Kate. Certainly the food here is fine, but can you think of a less romantic place to be?'

She did look round. Through the windows she could see the side of the kitchen, and a long line of bins. Inside, the canteen was stark, a place of plastic, linoleum and shadow-free light. It was clean, but... 'No, it's not romantic,' she said.

'So it's a good place to talk about romance. I like you a lot, Kate, and I think we are suited. You've told me you're one of Nature's wanderers, that this place can't hold you. When Jo has recovered, you'll be off. And I've given up all thoughts of a permanent relationship. Kate, we are made for each other.'

She was shocked at this. 'We are?' she asked.

'I think so, yes. We can bring each other great pleasure, and then, when the time comes, when you're off wandering again, we can part clean. There'll be regrets, of course, but I think we'll always be friends, even if we stop being lovers. Isn't that what you want?'

What he was saying made sense. But... 'I'm going to have to think,' she said slowly, 'but, yes, I suppose it is what I want.'

'Good. It's what I want too. I'm glad we agree.'

He had finished his salad. He took one last gulp of his tea, and stood. 'This is a doctor's life; I have to rush. You go out with John tonight and I'll phone you before you go. Incidentally—any time you phone me in future at the surgery you'll be connected at once.'

'That's a relief. I hope you didn't have a row with Vanessa?'

'No.' He stood looking down at her speculatively. 'If

I was John, I guess I'd bend over and try to kiss you now.'

'Well, you're not John and you can't. I've got better things to do than start gossip here. But you can kiss me tomorrow if you like.'

'Oh, I like,' he said, and then he was gone.

She pushed her unfinished salad aside. Unusually for her, she wasn't hungry.

She thought she had never found a man she liked as much as Steve. And he had outlined perfectly the kind of relationship she wanted—she needed. Too many men in her past had demanded permanence, had wanted love when all she'd been offering was friendship. But Steve understood how she felt. Everything seemed to be going fine. So why wasn't she happy?

When she got back to the A and E Margaret Welsh asked her—she didn't demand—if she could work lates for the rest of the week, including Saturday, and take Sunday and Monday off. She explained why she wanted to alter Kate's shifts. The reason was perfectly valid— a contract nurse had gone sick—so Kate said yes at once.

Though she tried not to show it, Margaret seemed a bit surprised at the readiness with which Kate agreed to her suggestion. 'I can manage,' Kate said. 'Our patients' needs come first. We have to be professional about this don't we?'

'Yes,' Margaret said heavily, 'we have to be professional.'

There was no more work counting stock for Kate.

Kate had phoned Jo's insurance company earlier in the day, and arranged cover so she could drive Jo's car. As soon as she got home from work she phoned John and suggested that he might like to take a drive round the countryside with her; he agreed at once and told her that he was thinking of spending a few days in London. 'Unless there's some special reason why I should stay here?' he asked hopefully.

'No, John, there isn't. But I'll drive you to the nearest station if you like.'

John seemed to accept the situation. She was changing before going round to pick him up at the Royal Lancaster when Steve rang up. It was only a few hours since she'd had lunch with him—and yet she was so pleased to hear his voice. There was an extra current in his voice too; she knew he was happy to be speaking to her.

She told him about changing her shifts and how she was to have Sunday and Monday off. Instantly, he was interested. 'That's good. I had a call from Dr Stanmore—you know, Amy's GP. The situation up there has got worse. Amy fell in the kitchen and sprained her ankle badly. When the nurse called she had been on the floor for a couple of hours, unable to get up. Dr Stanmore arranged for a home help to call in every day, but that was only a temporary thing. I thought we might go and see her again on Sunday, try to persuade her to move, and then go for another walk. D'you fancy that?'

'Very much so. It'll be nice to spend some time with you.'

'And with you, darling,' he said gently. 'Now—the real reason I rang. I'll see you tomorrow afternoon. It's just been arranged—I'm working in your A and E Department for half a shift.'

'The old team again! Great!' Life was being good to her.

*　　*　　*

In fact, they didn't see too much of each other. But it made her happy to see him in the corridor, to exchange smiles.

Sometimes work on the A and E unit was straight-forward. There weren't many exciting incidents in the afternoons. Little things, of course, like FBIs—Foreign Body in the Eye—that needed just irrigation and then reassurance. There were always plenty of cuts, some of which needed suturing, some of which didn't. There would be suspected wrist fractures that turned out to be sprains. There would be young men from the local college, still in running or athletic kit. Often the doctor had little to do but direct the nurse as to which dressing to put on.

But not always. Steve swished aside the curtain of the cubicle where she was bandaging a housewife's burned arm. 'Nearly finished?' he asked, his tone indicating that it would be a good idea if she were.

Kate nodded, then, 'That's fine now, Mrs Elsby,' she said. 'Take things easy for the rest of the day, and have the painkiller we gave you before you go to bed. Your GP can see to the rest of the treatment.' Mrs Elsby smiled and left.

'RTA coming in,' Steve said tersely, 'sounds like a bad one. Driver and the woman he knocked over. The driver's in shock, possible heart attack, the woman's in a bad state in general. I want you with me. I've sent for the rest of the trauma team.'

'I'm ready.' There were other nurses Steve could call on, but he tended to ask her. She knew it was because of her professional competence, not because he wanted to be with her.

They were waiting outside when the ambulance drew up. The paramedic gave her usual efficient summary.

'Driver's picking up. We've had the monitor on him, and his heart's settled down a bit. Apparently there's a history of low-grade heart trouble. But the woman's bad. Apparently she stepped out into the road, the car hit her and threw her against the kerb, she smashed her head on the pavement edge. She's bleeding, of course, but there could be brain damage too.'

Steve looked at the two as the man was hastened into a cubicle, the woman taken to the trauma room. The driver was now able to speak. Steve handed him over to a junior doctor with the instruction to take a history, make observations, and if anything seemed to be going seriously wrong to call him.

There was blood all over the woman. Kate took the handbag that had been on the stretcher and handed it to a junior nurse. 'Get someone to look through that with you, and see if you can find a name and a home address.' She remembered Holly Price the week before, but she had only been cut. This woman had possibly suffered serious trauma to the skull.

She helped Steve and the paramedics heave the woman onto the bed. Once she had been pretty, had taken care with her appearance. Now, the red slash of lipstick stood out against the chalk-white face. And there was blood everywhere—staining, ruining the once expensive green dress. On the fourth finger of the left hand was a wedding ring. Somewhere there was a husband.

This was a well-rehearsed procedure. There was now an anaesthetist, a neurologist, and an orthopaedics man in the room. The woman was attached to the cardiac monitor, and the anaesthetist slid an endo-tracheal tube down her throat and then he checked her eyes. There was the fixed dilated pupil that suggested bleeding in the skull.

'Giving set first,' Steve said. 'She needs plasma in her. In fact we'll have two lines.' The team was carrying out the usual battery of tests. Samples were taken, X-rays of spine, chest, skull and pelvis. Steve's fingers moved gently over the skull. 'There's a fracture there for certain.'

The vital signs were low. The pulse was thready and erratic, blood pressure drastically low. Kate cut off the blood-stained garments and threw them into a bucket, they were beyond repair. Steve bent over the naked body, looking for signs of injury other than the massive one to the head. He pointed to bruising and distortion in the left leg. Kate nodded. A broken tibia at least. But fortunately not as bad as Jo's.

The developed X-ray films were brought in and hung up. Everyone looked, and winced.

The shattered frame couldn't stand much more. The heartbeat fluttered, stopped and started again. Then the rhythm went haywire. Everyone looked at the monitor, watched the little green blip moving across the screen. The heart stopped.

First Steve tried cardiac pulmonary resusitation, pressing directly on the chest with his hands. There was no result. Then he drew up drugs as protocol, injected adrenaline and atropine into the heart. It did little good.

'We're going to have to shock her,' Steve said, and Kate fetched the clamps.

Three times the body jolted under the sudden current, but the woman remained in asystole. The heart wouldn't beat; the line was flat.

They tried for what seemed an endless time, repeating each procedure even though they knew it would do no good. But finally Steve sighed, and stepped back. 'Can anyone see any point in going on?' All there shook their heads. 'That's it, then. This one we have to lose. Thanks to all of you. We did what we could.'

A trainee nurse peered round the cubicle curtain. 'Her name's Eileen Dent. The police are here, and her husband and family are coming. They're...oh.' The silence suddenly struck her, the stillness of the body on the table.

Knowing the woman's name made her more of a person. She wasn't just a statistic any more. Kate looked at the white form below her as she started to take down the giving set. She had noticed before that when the soul left, when someone died, the body seemed to diminish too.

Steve said, 'We did all that could be done. Kate, could you...prepare the body so the family can see her? They don't have to see her like this.'

'I'll see to it,' said Kate. It wasn't a job she enjoyed, but she knew that Steve had a far worse one. Telling someone that a loved family member had suddenly been killed, was always traumatic. Any doctor who could do it easily was lacking in something. She went to fetch a bowl of warm water.

Driving home at the end of the shift, Kate felt rather melancholy. Steve had business back at the surgery; she was alone.

A young woman in the prime of her life, cut off so suddenly. She could never have anticipated this when she'd got up in the morning. What dreams had she had that now would never be realised?

Inevitably, this train of thought led Kate to think of herself. What did she want to do in life? Was she entirely happy with the way it was moving? Was there

something new she needed to do? She felt dissatisfied—
and now she knew why.

As soon as she got home she phoned Directory
Enquiries and found the number of Pendle View—the
retirement home that Dr Stanmore had recommended so
strongly. When she rang there, a cheerful, efficient-
sounding woman called Miss Bryce answered. Kate told
her that she was going to visit Amy Branwell next
Sunday, that she was a lady who had lived in the area
for the past twenty years, and Kate wondered if there
were any friends of hers in Pendle View.

'I'll go to find out,' the woman said. 'May I ring you
back?'

She did ring back, ten minutes later. She gave a list
of friends and acquaintances, all of whom would love
to see Amy again. One was even eager to play chess
with her.

She only managed to see Steve once before Sunday. He
called round on Saturday morning before she went on
to her shift. It was a bit unsatisfactory, but medical
workers were used to this kind of thing. They had a
coffee together, but that was all.

There had been a further problem. Jo wasn't to be
allowed out of hospital. She had contracted a fever, her
temperature had gone up and the consultant said that
she must stay in until she was healthier. Kate had
looked forward to her coming home. She suspected that
the hospital environment, where everything was done
for her, was only giving her sister time to mope over
her past troubles.

But Sunday morning came, and as before it was so
good to see him.

'What's that?' he asked as she carefully loaded a round brown pot into his car boot.

'It's a beef casserole; I made it last night. I thought Amy might like a warm meal. I don't know how many she's been having.' She dropped in a silver-covered parcel and a Thermos. 'And I made a few sandwiches for us, and filled a flask with tea.'

He looked at her reflectively. 'You're a nice person, Kate Wilde.'

He pointed to a bag on the back seat. 'I'm not sure about the weather, it feels as it there might be a storm to me. So I've put in a change of clothing, just in case I get wet. D'you want to do the same?'

So she ran upstairs and packed a small bag with underwear, socks and trainers, and a tracksuit. It would do if she got soaked.

She enjoyed the drive north again, but they had to have the windows fully open. She had to admit that Steve was right about the weather. It was very warm, but very close. When they finally got out of the car her shirt was sticking to her back, and she could see the beads of sweat along his hairline. The sun was out, but very dim, and a thick haze made it seem difficult to breathe. Even walking down to Amy's front door made them both sweat.

Amy was very pleased to see them, but obviously feeling the heat herself. Kate knew from her experiences in Las Vegas that old people could have greater difficulty coping with heat than with cold. 'We've brought a casserole,' she said, 'but before we eat it would you like a tepid bath? It might make you feel better.'

Amy agreed that it might be a good idea, so she had a bath. Kate thought that the old lady was, if anything, a bit thinner than before. 'You must eat more,' she said. 'You've got to keep your strength up.'

'I get so I just can't be bothered preparing anything,' said Amy.

Afterwards they had the casserole, and Amy seemed to be a little more lively. 'I do feel better for that,' she said. 'I feel brighter.'

'Brighter? Leonie Fletcher said she wouldn't mind another game of chess with you,' Kate said. 'Apparently she often used to beat you.'

'No, she didn't—ever,' snapped Amy. 'Well, perhaps once or twice.'

'And Jamie Kerrigan was asking about your garden. He said he used to visit you a lot.'

'How do you know my friends?'

'And I've got messages for you from Lucie Donovan and Pat Kimble. They'd all love to see more of you.'

Amy looked at Steve. 'She's setting me up for something, isn't she?' she asked.

He answered straight-faced. 'I suspect so. And she usually gets her own way too.'

'You know they all live in Pendle View, that residential home in the village,' Kate said gently. 'They all see a lot of each other. They'd love to see you there too. Why don't you move in there for a fortnight—say while your ankle gets better? You could call it respite. Then you could come back here if you wanted to.'

'Did Steve and that GP of mine put you up to this?'

'No,' said Steve, 'this is the first I've heard of it. But I do think it's a good idea.'

'Hmm.' There was silence for a moment, then, 'Well, I suppose I could try it for a week or two.'

Trying desperately to be casual, Kate said, 'Why not let Steve use his mobile phone to ring Dr Stanmore, who'll see if it's all right for you just to drop in? Then I could help you pack a few things.'

'It seems like a good idea. But we'll have our tea first. Shall we go in the garden?'

They sat in the shade as Steve phoned a delighted Dr Stanmore. Amy looked over the valley and said, 'You're a wanderer Steve tells me.'

'Yes. At the moment I'm looking after my sister, but when she's better I shall be on my way again.'

'Looking for anything special?'

'If I am, I don't know what it is, and I certainly haven't found it yet.'

'Hmm. I've looked at this view every morning for twenty years. Perhaps it's time I looked at something else.'

'There's a river behind the home,' Kate said, 'and a beautiful garden. It'll be good to look at something else.'

'Perhaps it would be good for you to stop wandering.'

'I've been thinking that myself,' Kate said, and then was surprised at the admission.

Steve came to say that Dr Stanmore had phoned back. There was a place for Amy and everyone was looking forward to seeing her. 'Let's go and pack, then,' said Amy.

'You'll be coming here again,' Kate said. 'You don't have to say goodbye to the place. You're only going to Pendle View for a fortnight.'

'I'm not a fool, Kate. Perhaps I might come back one last time, but that will be all. We both know I'm going to this place for good. But I shall miss my hilltop home.'

She said this so wistfully that Kate felt her eyes fill with tears.

'Don't be sentimental, girl,' snapped Amy. 'Everything has to change, and often it's for the better. Let's go and pack.'

CHAPTER EIGHT

'WE DON'T have much time for a walk,' Steve said some four hours later, 'and even though the afternoon is getting on, I don't fancy climbing hills in this heat. It was bad enough carrying parcels and cases. What about an easy stroll along the river?'

'Lead me to it,' Kate said, 'and a bit of shade would be a good idea.'

They had both been surprised at how happily Amy had adapted to the change. Dr Stanmore had arranged the room, Kate had helped Amy pack, and Steve had made sure the cottage was safe to be left. Then they had bumped slowly down the path and on to the little road to Bramley.

Kate had noticed that when they'd set off Amy had resolutely refused to look back. She'd caught Kate watching at her. 'This is going to be a beginning, not an end,' she'd said. 'I'm looking forward.'

When they'd got to the home there had been a little afternoon party waiting for her, and a chessboard ready for a game. Amy had been at home at once, and Steve and Kate had left quickly.

'You've done a super job,' Steve said now. 'There's a side of you that I knew was there but I'd not seen before.'

'What about my walk?' she asked.

It was pleasant by the river. At first they walked through a park—and he bought her an ice cream which made them more thirsty than ever. But then they were on the narrow riverside path, sometimes shaded, sometimes not. They passed the place where last time they had turned upwards, and smiled at each other. Too hot for that now.

She made him put on sunblock again, and they walked onwards. It was hot, so hot that other walkers had decided not to bother. They met no one, they seemed to be alone in the world. After a while the walls of the valley drew in and they moved in single file along a path carved out of the banks of the river.

Eventually they came to the end of the valley. Ahead of them was a wall of large boulders with a waterfall splashing down it. 'We'll get to the top there,' Steve said, wiping the sweat from his face, 'and then we'll call it a day.'

It wasn't a hard climb, there was a well-defined route to the top, and there they found a pool. It was a little blue gem, surrounded by acres of empty green moorland. There were sheep there, but no people.

'It's beautiful,' she cried. 'It looks really inviting. I'd love a dip.' She pulled her damp shirt away from her sticky body. 'There's no one around. I think I'll swim in my knickers.'

'Or swim out of them,' he said. 'Then you'll have something dry to put on afterwards.'

She turned her back to undress, so it came as a shock when his naked body leaped past her and dived into the pool. 'You could have told me you had nothing on,' she said primly.

He swam to the centre of the pool, then rolled over on his back and looked at her. 'This is so good,' he said. 'Aren't you going to come in?'

'A gentleman would turn his back while I got undressed,' she offered.

'But I want to watch. I got undressed in front of you. If you're too modest, then hide behind that bush.'

Well, he hadn't exactly got undressed in front of her, but this still was a challenge. She sat to take her boots and socks off. Then her shirt and bra, and in one movement her trousers and knickers. A split second later she too had leaped into the water. The initial shock took her breath away. But then it was as good, as refreshing as he'd said.

She swam across to him. The top layer of water was quite warm, but when she dived she found that underneath it was deliciously cool. She surfaced, looking at him with his hair slicked down. He looked as wonderful as always.

They were close now, and she stood, her feet just touching the bottom. He surged forward, put his arms round her, pulled her close to him. She felt his naked body pressed against hers, cool but strangely exciting. He kissed her. This too was odd, but exciting. Her breasts were crushed against his chest and she could feel his masculinity against her thigh.

She sighed. 'This is…different,' she said.

'Different, perhaps. But is it good?'

'You know it is.' Her head and shoulders were out of the water; she could feel the heat of the sun on them. The rest of her was cool. His lips too were cool on hers, but still exciting. 'Let's swim,' she said.

After a while they climbed out. First they looked round, but the fells were as deserted as ever. So they lay down side by side. By now there was no false modesty between them. She looked at his slimly muscled body, and knew that he was taking note of hers. Both were medical people anyway; they were used to naked bodies. Yet this was different.

They soon dried in the sun, but their bodies were now cool. She lay on her back, eyes closed, completely relaxed. Something told her that things between them would soon change, that their lives would alter. It was to be, and she was happy with it.

The grass rustled. She felt his thigh rub and twist against hers. The warmth of the sun on her body was suddenly cut off; he was leaning over her. The nearness of him poised above her was electric. She felt that she couldn't wait for him to lie on her; her body ached for his weight. But only his lips came down to touch hers. Gently at first, he kissed her, the softest of feather touches. Then she moaned, a soft call to him, and his mouth pressed harder on hers. It was so good.

But she wanted more, and when he pulled away her eyes flashed open, hurt, demanding. 'What are you doing?' she muttered. 'Come back to me.' She gazed at his face, desperate with desire.

He leaned back, pointed to a thick copse of fir trees, some twenty yards away. 'Let's go there,' he said, 'D'you want to come with me, Kate?'

She said nothing, but scrambled to her feet and grabbed a handful of clothes. Then, naked, but with their arms round each other, they walked to the shelter of the little copse.

It was dark among the trees. There was the heady scent of pine and the needles underfoot had the softness of a pillow. He spread his shirt out for her and they knelt, facing each other. Now they could embrace; as he kissed her she felt the muscles of his chest crushing her breasts, the evidence of his need for her hard against her thigh.

Gently he lowered her onto her back. There was a moment whilst he fumbled in the pocket of his shirt, and then he was above her again, and she reached out for him, her entire being aching for him. There was a moment's discomfort, easily ignored, and she found herself with him, moving with a primeval rhythm that came instinctively to them both. Both knew there was no time for long drawn-out preliminaries; their need for each other was too great. She sensed his growing urgency, shared in it herself, and them screamed aloud, matching the hoarseness of his groan of ecstasy.

For a while they said nothing, content to lie there in each other's arms. Then they dressed, and lazily ate her sandwiches and drank the Thermos of tea. There was no need for words; being together was communion enough. Then they stretched out again. 'I'm sleepy,' she said. 'How about you?'

'Well, I don't feel like walking yet.'

So she rested her head on his shoulder, he wrapped his arms round her and together they slept.

There was something moving over her face. She knew it wasn't an insect so she didn't mind too much. She was in a blissful half-sleep, aware of something of the world around her but not wanting to wake and cope with any problems.

Then the something moving over her face kissed her, and she had to wake up. There was Steve looking down at her. 'I think we're going to have rain,' he said. 'Perhaps we should be getting back.'

She looked beyond him to the sky. The sun had gone in and the sky was darker, hazier. If anything it was even warmer, and the stillness full of foreboding.

'I know we've got waterproofs,' he said, 'but I still think we should hurry back. It's going to pour down.'

Slowly, she sat upright, yawned. 'Probably a good idea. I enjoyed that little sleep. Did you sleep too?'

'Perhaps a bit. But most of the time I just looked at you.'

She didn't know what to say to this. Certainly she didn't yet want to talk about what they had just done. It was too close, too wonderful. Rolling to her feet, she said, 'I think you're right about the weather. Let's go.'

They climbed back down the little wall of boulders and set off down the meandering path by the river. At first it was warm—but very quickly it grew colder. There was the first hint of a chill wind, and the sky got even darker. They stopped and pulled on their waterproofs. As they did so there were the first loud smacks as heavy raindrops slapped onto them. Two minutes later there was a sound like paper tearing, and they saw a grey wall of rain advancing towards them along the valley.

'Shelter,' he shouted to her. 'Let's get under those trees.' They both ran to another little copse of pine trees and huddled underneath as the rain suddenly pelted down.

He put his arms round her shoulders and peered into her drawn-up hood. 'This will slacken after a bit, and then we'll walk back,' he told her. 'Are you OK?'

It was cosy, squatting together with their backs to the turpentine-smelling tree. She thought of what had happened not an hour before and smiled happily at the memory before replying to him. 'I'm fine,' she told him. 'In fact I quite like this. We don't get much rain in Las Vegas.'

'I'm surprised you get any. Isn't it in the desert?'

'It never used to rain in Las Vegas. In fact it was so dry that they never bothered putting drains in the streets.

But sometimes now it does rain, and the streets flood. And in the desert we're always told to watch out if you're in one of those narrow valleys. If there's a flash flood higher up, you can get ten feet of water coming down in a great wave.'

'I'll stick to Britain,' he said. 'Isn't it nice to have a pointless conversation when you're getting wet through?'

'I'm enjoying it,' she told him.

After ten minutes the initial deluge eased up and settled into a steady downpour that looked as if it would continue for the rest of the day. 'Might as well set off,' he said. 'We're going to get wet even with our waterproofs, but we've got something dry to change into back at the car.'

'You lead; I'll follow.' Heads down, they set off down the valley.

The ground was now very slippery; the sudden rain had made it greasy. Runnels of mud crossed the path and both of them slipped a couple of times. Kate walked after Steve, there still wasn't room to walk side by side. Her shoulders were hunched, her head bent, and the rain pattered off her—but she was happy. This weather made a change.

Suddenly he stopped and she walked into him. As she watched, he pushed back his hood and turned his head, frowning. The rain flattened his hair. 'What is it?' she asked. 'Did you hear something?'

'I thought I did. But I'm not sure.'

Now she pushed back her hood, and the two of them listened intently. There was a momentary lull in the pattering of rain on their waterproofs, and both heard the same thing. Far off in the distance, a solitary word— 'Help!'

Steve pointed up the side of the hill. 'It seemed to come from up there. Let's go and see.' Together they scrambled up the steep side of the valley, sliding on the wet grass and mud. It was hard, hot work.

After a while the hillside flattened out a little. There was a field, cut into the side of the hill. On the far edge of the field, where the hill rose steeply again, there was a farm track. And by it, lying on its side, was a tractor.

It was easy to see what had happened. The farm track was built up above the field, and underneath the tractor was a fan of fresh mud; the side of the built-up track had collapsed under the weight of the tractor, the tractor had slid and then rolled over. And pinned below the tractor, only his head and shoulders visible, was a man.

'Help me,' came his weak voice, his despairing voice, only just audible over the sound of the rain.

The two ran towards him. Kate looked around. There was no one else in sight, no sign of farm or cottage nearby. This they would have to deal with on their own.

Hearts hammering with the exertion, they came up to the tractor, slipping even more in the fresh mud below it. 'We'll have to watch it,' Steve gasped, 'it's not impossible that the tractor might roll again. Don't want to be underneath.' But he still headed straight for the man.

After one quick glance they both knew that they were going to need help. The man was trapped, caught between the ground and a firmly fixed steel strut that pressed into his chest. Kate knelt by him, took his hand. 'OK, we're here now; we'll get something done. I'm a nurse and this man is a doctor. We'll do what we can for you. What's your name?'

'Ray...Ray Jenkins,' the man gasped. 'I thought no one would ever come.'

'Well, we're here now.' She knew there might not be

much they could do, but it was essential to reassure the man. By now he would be going into shock.

Steve took out his mobile. 'I'll phone for an ambulance and the fire brigade,' he said. 'We're going to need jacks or something to get him loose.'

She watched him dial 999, and saw the signal flash on the screen—searching for a network. He moved upwards a little, tried again, the same thing happened. From the ground, the man gasped, 'You'll never get through from here—the valley's too tight round you. Only way...only way is get to top of the fell.'

Kate looked upwards through the sheeting rain. The hillside rose steeply above her, the top out of sight. 'Give me your mobile,' she told Steve. 'I'll run up there and get through.'

No time for hampering waterproofs now. She pulled off her jacket, clutched the mobile in her hand and staggered upwards.

It was hard work. Three or four times she fell, sliding backwards across the slippery grass, with only one hand to save herself. Her heart had been pounding before, now she thought she had never felt it beat so fast. But eventually the gradient eased off, and then she reached the fell summit. She dialled 999, looked at the little screen. There was a signal.

It was ever harder trying to control her rasping breathing, but she managed. The operator was clear and understanding. Kate explained where they were, the nature of the accident and that they would need an ambulance and perhaps some kind of lifting apparatus. Then she skidded back down the hillside.

Ray was unconscious now. Steve had wrapped him in his silver space blanket, to try to stop his body temperature falling—hypothermia was a risk. Kate tucked her own silver blanket further down his body. Every little might help. Then she looked to see what Steve was doing.

He had built little walls between the tractor and the ground, jamming stones in the gap so that the tractor would not sink further into the sodden ground and crush Ray to death. Now he was using his bare hands to dig at the mud underneath the man. 'If we can loosen this earth and pull it out we might be able to ease him downwards, perhaps even slide him out,' he panted. 'I'm scared the tractor might settle further. Just another couple of inches and he would have been dead already.'

She moved to the other side of Ray's body, started to dig in her turn, scooping wet earth and pebbles from under Ray's body and throwing it behind her. Dimly, she realised she was filthy. There was mud everywhere. 'What happened?' she asked. 'I thought tractors were supposed to be safe now. I thought this bar that's holding him down was supposed to protect him.'

'It would have protected him,' Steve said gloomily, 'if he'd stayed put. But I guess he felt the tractor starting to roll and tried to jump free. He was very lucky he wasn't crushed instantly.'

She felt Ray's body slump downwards just a couple of inches, almost trapping her arm. 'I think he might be free now,' she said. 'Shall we try to pull him out?'

It was a hard question to answer. They didn't know what crush injuries Ray might have sustained. Pulling at his body now might do irreparable damage. As well as possible broken bones, the spleen, the pancreas, the duodenum, the liver—all could have been injured. Ideally they would have liked the tractor jacked upwards, so they could make an examination without moving the patient. But this wasn't an ideal situation. The tractor could sink further.

'We pull him out,' said Steve. 'We don't really have an option.'

As gently as they could, they eased the body from under the tractor. There was a further problem in carrying him away from it. He needed the flatness of a stretcher. Kate saw an old sheet of corrugated iron, wired to the bottom of a gate. After pointing it out to Steve, she ran over and pulled it away. She and Steve were able to slide it under the unconscious Ray, and then slide him across the grass, away from the tractor.

She wrapped the silver blankets even more firmly round Ray while Steve checked ABC again. Then there was nothing to do but wait. Steve carried a small first aid kit, but it was useless for this kind of emergency. If Ray's breathing stopped they would be able to give him mouth to mouth resuscitation. But they would not dare try any kind of cardiac massage. They had no idea how badly injured his chest was.

'What I wouldn't give for an A and E room!' Steve groaned. 'We've got him out, Kate, but we're missing the Golden Hour. Every minute now his chances of survival are getting less.'

'I know,' she said. The Golden Hour was the time immediately after a massive trauma, when prompt medical aid could often save a patient's life. Almost certainly Ray was bleeding internally. He needed attention *now*!

For a moment she thought about how things would be in her department. Arterial line up, a baseline gas done, chest drain readied, chest X-ray, blood sent for cross-matching. All in a matter of minutes.

Then she heard the rumble of engines, and on the far

side of the field she saw flashing blue lights appearing through the murk. Two vehicles appeared—a police Land Rover and a similar vehicle equipped as an ambulance. They drove cautiously forward, stopped well away from the tractor, and blue and green-clad figures leaped out. 'Now we can hand over to the professionals,' Steve said.

The two paramedics trotted over and she heard Steve give an incisive report, just as the paramedics would when they handed their charge over to the A and E department. Then she and Steve stood back, as did the policemen. This was an emergency situation, not a medical one. These men were trained for it.

Ray was eased gently onto a stretcher, loaded into the ambulance. Then a paramedic looked at the two of them. 'You two OK? Any injuries, any falls?'

'We're cold, wet and dirty,' Steve said. 'But otherwise we're fine.'

'When you get back, get yourself checked out,' the man suggested. 'You never know what you might have missed.' He turned to one of the policemen. 'Soon as we're in contact we'll cancel the fire brigade, Martin. They're not needed now.' The policeman nodded.

The ambulance slowly drove away. 'I think we'd better give you two a lift,' the policeman called Martin said. 'Take you somewhere you can dry off. We'd like a statement at some time, but there's no hurry. You've done a good job. Ray Jenkins there would have died but for you.'

'Just lucky we were there,' Steve said.

It was warm in the police Land Rover, and Kate shuddered as Steve put his arm round her. Reaction was setting in. She had been fine while there were things to do, but now she realised she was tired, scratched, bruised and muddy. She also wondered if she was going to cry.

'I've got a suggestion,' Steve said quietly. 'There's a big hotel in the centre of the village, an old posting inn called the Farrell Arms. How about trying to stay there the night? We could have a bath, a meal, get into our dry clothes.'

The thought of a bath was almost too blissful to bear. 'Right,' she said. 'We'll share a room, won't we?'

'Of course,' he said.

Martin, the police constable, offered to make things easy for them. He ran them round to the Farrell Arms, and went in to explain things to the manager. The manager came out to see them. 'Ray Jenkins is a regular,' he said. 'For helping him you can have the best room in the house. And I'll borrow you a dressing gown each. Can I send you something up to eat?'

Martin said, 'If you give me your car keys I'll have the car fetched round. Then I've got to get in touch with Ray's family. Can you drop in tomorrow and make a short statement?'

Both Steve and Kate had insisted that they take their boots off before they walked across the red carpet and up to their wondrously warm room. 'You bath first,' said Steve.

She stood in the centre of the bathroom and surveyed herself in the full-length mirror there. She was a wreck! Her hair was plastered tight to her skull, except where the mud had lifted it in little ridges. There were runnels of bright pink down through the mud on her cheeks, where tears had run. Her once reasonably-smart casual clothes were filthy. And she was dog-tired—and she didn't care.

The bath was large and old-fashioned. She ran it till the steam rose, and dropped in packets of sweet-smelling salts. It was an effort to peel off her clothes, and she left them in a muddy heap in the middle of the floor. Then she swished the water round till it was covered in thick white foam, and only then did she lower herself into it. Bliss! Was there any pleasure greater than a hot bath when you were cold, dirty and weary? She sank under the water until only her face was visible. This was glorious. She could stay here for ever.

After a while there was a tap on the door and Steve's voice called, 'May I come in?' She considered hiding her modesty with the flannel, but decided it was too late—besides, the foam would do. So she told him to come in.

He was still muddy, but had taken off his shirt and socks. Standing there, stripped to the waist, he looked like some Viking marauder. So she was surprised when, putting a large cup on the side of the bath, he said, 'I'm a ladies' maid. Here's your tea, with a tot of whisky added, and a bathrobe. I'll hang it on the door. This basket is to put your wet clothes in—' he stooped to pick them up '—and I'm to give them to the chamber maid who will see what she can do with them by tomorrow morning. And a little presentation pack each, with toothbrush, razor, that sort of thing.'

'They seem to be going to a lot of trouble for us,' Kate said, surprised.

'I gather we're local heroes. This man Ray Jenkins is apparently very popular, very well known. Now, you drink your tea, and I'm going to do a bit of telephoning. I'd better let people know where I am.'

'Vanessa isn't going to be very pleased to know you're here with me,' Kate said cattily.

'Vanessa will just have to get over it. Anyway, I'm going to phone Jerry Cash, one of my partners. Drink your tea!'

She could have stayed in the bath for ever. But the thought of Steve waiting made her get out, rinse her hair under the shower and then wrap towel and robe round her. 'Your turn,' she said. 'I'm going to sit here and dry my hair.'

He disappeared into the bathroom; she sat in a comfortable armchair and tried to relax. But she had relaxed enough in the bath. Now she had to take stock. She had made decisions about her life, about Steve. Did she want to stick to them?

A clock on the wall told her that it was now nine o'clock. It was still light outside. She saw her bag of clean, dry clothes, brought from the car, on the table. Quickly she pulled on her tracksuit. Now she was dressed, she was less—vulnerable?

If necessary they could still drive home tonight. She felt an awful lot better, and she guessed that Steve would too, and if she asked he wouldn't mind driving her back. But he had suggested that they stay the night, and she had suggested that they share a room. She looked at the twin beds at the far end of the room.

Kate poured herself some more tea, drank it, and thought. Then she tapped on the bathroom door herself and went inside. Steve was doing just what she had done, revelling in the hot water.

'We've got twin beds,' she said. 'But we could move the cabinet out from between them and push them together.'

Gently, he said, 'That's the best thing anyone has ever said to me while I was having a hot bath. Wait till I get out.'

She was in her tracksuit; he was wearing a sweater and old jeans. They decided they weren't dressed to go down to the dining room, and the manager was more than willing to serve a meal upstairs. So they ate heartily—locally cured gammon with salad, and then Wensleydale cheese. With it, of course, their usual favourite bottle of dry red wine.

When they had finished, and the waiter was clearing the plates away, the manager came in and brought them another bottle. It came with the compliments of the management, and with some good news. Ray Jenkins had been operated on for a ruptured spleen, but was now out of danger. 'They said that if he had been under that tractor for another quarter of an hour he would have died,' the manager said soberly. 'He owes you his life.'

'We were just there,' Steve said. 'Anyone would have done the same.'

They had another glass of wine each, and sat quietly as it got dark. They didn't bother to put on the light, just listened to the rain rattling on the window panes, the mutter of conversation from the lounge below. There was no couch, just two armchairs, so after a while she stood and went to kneel between his legs. His hands touched her hair, stroked her shoulders. She was comfortable there.

Eventually it was fully dark. 'I'm tired. It's time for bed,' she said.

CHAPTER NINE

KATE *was* tired, more tired than she had realised, and guessed that Steve was too. But inside her there was an anticipation building. They had made love not too many hours before, but in a frenzy of excitement. This would be different.

He helped her carry the cabinet away from the between the two beds, and then pull out the sheets. There was no point in their being in touching beds if they couldn't reach for each other. She left on just one bedside light.

Then she stood in front of him and quickly pulled off her clothes. He undressed equally quickly.

They didn't get into bed at first, instead he came over to her and held her by the shoulders. He looked at her. His eyes were in shadow, but she could tell his emotion by the curve of his lips. Gently, he pulled her to him. There was something exciting and different about being hugged, standing up, by a naked man. She felt as if all of him was pressing against her. Their knees touched, their thighs rubbed together, and with her breasts she could feel the hair on his chest. Their arms were round each other. And she could feel his desire for her.

For a while they just stood there, cheek to cheek, not even kissing. She could smell the shampoo and soap on him and feel the warmth of his body. She wriggled a bit, it was so nice. And that made her more aware of his growing need for her.

She tugged him, and, arms round each other's waists,

they walked to the bed. She lay on her back and looked up into his eyes, smoky with desire. His longing for her was so great she could sense it.

He leaned over and kissed her then—a long, sensuous kiss, exploring the sweetness of her mouth and lips. Her arms slid round him, easing him down onto her, so she could rejoice, take pleasure in his weight on her. And take pleasure in his ever-growing excitement.

His lips moved down her body, across her neck, the bones of her shoulders, the swell of her breasts. Then her body arched as he took each pink tip into his mouth. His tongue grazed, touched, teased, his mouth squeezed. This was exquisite agony!

Kate felt her breathing deepen, knew the rapid beating of her heart—and his. This was so much—and yet this was only the beginning. She opened herself to him.

With one hand she felt for him, delighting at his groan of pleasure. Then he came nearer to her, touched her, there.

Now there was no stopping his growing excitement, nor hers. Instinctively, she knew what to do. Together they joined in a growing climax, to culminate in ecstasy.

For a moment they lay, side by side, chests heaving, skin glistening. 'That was so good,' she murmured. 'I think I love you, Steve.'

Next morning it was fine. Kate woke to see sunlight shining through the sides of the curtains, to hear the distant song of birds. When she looked at Steve, his face was curiously childlike, even though it was shadowed by the darkness of his beard.

Kate didn't kiss him because she didn't want to wake him. Instead she carefully slipped out of bed, put on her dressing gown and tiptoed over to the window. It was a gorgeous morning but the streets were still wet.

Quietly she phoned Room Service and asked for tea for two. When it came she poured two cups and walked back to where the two beds were still pushed together. A drowsy voice said, 'Did I hear the tinkle of a teaspoon? That's the best sound in the world when you wake in the morning.'

She put the tea on his bedside table and leaned over to kiss him. 'And that's the best feeling in the world,' he said.

'Sit up and drink your tea.'

They sat side by side in bed, drinking their tea. Kate looked at him, Now he was awake he was frowning. 'Why're you looking so worried?' she asked. 'We're supposed to be happy. What's the problem?'

He didn't stop frowning. 'Last night was wonderful,' he said. 'But this is the next morning and we have to...'

She leaned over to kiss him. 'We don't have to do anything. We're friends and we're lovers. You don't want to get married, and after a while I'll be away again. Until then we can bring each other happiness, and part with no regrets. Right?'

He still didn't seem convinced. But then he put down his cup, and said, 'I'm sure you're right. And as for bringing each other happiness...' She giggled as he pressed her back down onto the bed.

They still had a lot to do. They went downstairs for breakfast, and afterwards Steve queried the far too low bill. They promised to return quite soon as they had enjoyed their stay. Then they drove round to the little police station and gave a quick report. They were told that Ray Jenkins was doing well; he would write to them later. Then they took the road for home.

'Quite an eventful couple of days,' he said as they passed Pendle View. 'Interesting, exciting—but I wouldn't want to do it every Sunday and Monday.'

'None of it?' Kate asked. 'I can think of a couple of highlights.'

'Well, those we could repeat,' he said judiciously. 'But in general—well, we need to do some thinking.'

'I suppose you're right,' she said. 'Can we have some music on?'

She found his tape of Elton John again, and enjoyed listening to the mix of joyous and sad music. And she thought. She leaned over, rested her hand on Steve's thigh. He smiled at her. 'Why don't you try to sleep?' he asked. 'You didn't get all that much last night.'

'Whose fault was that?' Then she blushed. 'I suppose it was mine as much as anyone's, wasn't it?'

He reached down and squeezed her hand.

So Kate reclined her seat and shut her eyes. She didn't want to sleep; she wanted to think.

Last night and this morning had been wonderful. Steve was a thoughtful, considerate, passionate lover— all she could have wished for. And he hadn't made any emotional demands. He didn't try to be possessive like John, he knew that in time they would part. That was what she had said she wanted. So why did she feel strangely dissatisfied? Just reaction, she told herself.

Then an unwelcome thought forced itself through. Something she had tried to ignore, forget. Last night she had said to Steve, 'I think I love you.' He hadn't replied, hadn't questioned her, and for that she was glad. But she had never said it before to any man.

*　　*　　*

When she went to visit her sister that afternoon she was told that Jo would be discharged from hospital the following night. Kate went straight down to A and E and explained to Margaret Welsh that she would only be able to work days for the rest of the week, Jo would need her in the evenings. Margaret was surprisingly willing to accept this, and said she would rearrange the duty rosters. She even said that Kate could take half a day off. 'All I ask is that you let me know when you are able to work any shift—day or night.'

'I'll certainly do that,' Kate said. 'You're being very helpful, and I'm ever so grateful.'

'Not at all,' sniffed Margaret. 'We may have had our disagreements, but I regard you as a very competent nurse. The department needs your skills.'

Kate still wondered what had brought about the change of heart.

That evening Steve phoned and apologised; he just couldn't make it this evening. To her surprise, ten minutes later Andrew Kirk phoned her to discuss Jo's homecoming.

'If she keeps her mobile with her at all times,' Kate said, 'then she can easily call me if there's any emergency.'

Andrew looked at her quizzically. 'In time she'll have to stand on her own feet. I mean that both physically and mentally. You mustn't try to stand between her and all the evils of the world.'

Kate nodded. 'I know that. But she needs a couple of weeks' more tender loving care before she has to face up to the rest of her life. And the physiotherapy is going to be hard.'

'True. And in a sense her stay in hospital has been a

bit of a break from reality. In hospital you make few of your own decisions. Now she's going to start thinking for herself again. And she's going to start grieving for Harry again, worrying and wondering what she did wrong. There might be a period of depression.'

Kate nodded again. With working always in A and E, she saw little of the problems of long-term patient care. Her sister would need looking after.

Next day she *did* come home early from the hospital, and rushed round the house again, putting flowers in vases, rearranging the couch and chairs, making sure there was the good smell of percolating coffee coming from the kitchen.

Then the phone rang. It was a call she hadn't expected. 'It's John,' the voice explained. 'Kate, I'm back from London a little earlier than I intended.'

No, Kate thought. Right now I just can't deal with John. I've got other, bigger, better problems. But before she could say anything, he continued, 'I thought it only right to tell you. Tonight I'm taking Vanessa Welsh out to dinner. I hope you don't mind.'

'Taking Vanessa out to dinner? You are? Er—of course I don't mind, John.' She didn't mind. She was just completely dumbfounded.

'She has the right attitude to medicine; she's a very serious, person. I've—er—phoned her every night. We have a lot in common. But I didn't want you to…'

'No, that's fine, John. You take Vanessa to dinner.'

She could hear him sigh with relief. 'I'm glad we've got that sorted. We really must remain friends. I've had a long talk with Vanessa, and she absolutely agrees with me. In fact we'd like to invite you and Steve to dinner. Just the four of us. Shall I phone him and suggest it?'

'Yes,' said Kate faintly. 'I'm sure he'll be—delighted.'

'Then I'll phone you back with a suggested date. Bye, Kate, and thanks for being so understanding.' He rang off.

Kate stood there for a moment, unable to think. John and Vanessa? Was the world going mad? Then she realised that the two had quite a lot in common. They took themselves and their work very, very seriously indeed. And neither had a sense of humour. They could be made for each other.

Just before Jo was due to come home Andrew Kirk turned up, this time with his wife and his new senior registrar, Ben Franklin. 'We'll stay exactly five minutes,' Andrew said. 'Just enough time for her to know that there are people she can call on.'

'And people who need her back at work,' Ben said. 'That is, people like me. Without Jo, Andrew is evil in the theatre. A slave-driver. We need Jo to cool him down.'

Andrew beamed happily at this. 'There could be some truth in that remark,' he said.

Andrew's wife Penny was a pleasant, grey-haired lady with a soft voice. Kate had spoken to her two or three times on the telephone, but this was the first time they had met. She liked Penny at once. There was an air of quiet efficiency about her, and Kate suspected she was more than a match for the ebullient Andrew.

Ben had only just joined the team; Jo had said she knew little of him. But Kate took to him at once. His hair was longer than the short brutal style that was currently modish, and she admired a man who could stand up to fashion. And he seemed to care. There was a warmth, an empathy about him that she liked.

The ambulance drew up outside, and Jo was carefully shepherded into the living room, placed on the couch with a long stool ready to support her plastered leg. She was obviously pleased to be back, but just the short journey from hospital had tired her. Very quickly Andrew, Penny and Ben left, promising to come whenever they were needed.

'Come and hug me, little sister,' Jo said, and Kate kneeled by the side of the couch and did so. She could feel the wetness of Jo's tears running down her cheek.

'I just don't know what I would have done without you, Kate,' Jo said. 'You've made my life bearable. The others have been fine, but you're the one I need.' She pushed Kate back so she could look at her. 'You're not going back to America yet, are you?'

'Of course not.' Kate hugged Jo again. 'I'll be here as long as you want me. I've got a good job in A and E; I'm getting on well there. I wouldn't dream of leaving until you're fed up with me.'

'I'll never be that; you know very well. I'm so glad you're staying—if you can, just for a week or two. But I don't want you to stay here longer just for me.'

'One, I will stay here longer, just for you. You know you'd do the same for me. And two, it doesn't matter. I've no great wish to set off wandering again. I'm enjoying life round here too much.'

Jo knew her sister well. 'You actually meant that, I could tell,' she said. 'Apart from me, there must be some other, some special reason.' She frowned. 'You've been seeing a lot of Steve, haven't you?'

Kate shrugged elaborately. 'He's turned into a good friend,' she said, 'and he's been very helpful when I didn't know what to do with you.'

She couldn't hide anything from her sister. 'I think

he's more than a good friend,' Jo said. She thought a minute and then went on, 'Don't forget I know the family. I was going to marry Steve's cousin. I thought he'd make me happy for the rest of my life, and look what happened. Harry was so easy to love, Kate, and I'll bet Steve is too. I hope you don't make the same mistake as I did.'

'You need to think about something else,' Kate said, not wanting her sister to know how effective her words had been. 'Now, we'll talk in a minute about the programme the physio has given you, but for the moment let's see what's on telly. I'm going to get you a regular supply of videos for when I'm not here. D'you think you'll be able to manage without me? I can always give up work.'

'Wouldn't dream of you giving up work,' Jo said. 'If you're working here you're likely to stay longer. You make some tea and I'll play with the TV remote.'

Kate was glad to escape into the kitchen; she needed to think a moment in peace. What Jo had said had shocked her. Was Steve at all like Harry? Certainly they looked alike—was their behaviour likely to be similar? Would she fall into the same trap as Jo had?

Of course, their situations were different. It was clearly understood between Steve and herself that anything they had was not to be permanent. In time they would part, hopefully as good friends. There was no trap there. That was the difference between her and Jo.

Only when she had prepared the tea tray did she remember something that an old nurse had told her, many years ago when she had still been training. A young doctor had invited her to the Christmas Dance and, although she'd quite liked him, she had turned him down. There had been another doctor—slightly older—who had hinted that he would take her. But he'd never got round to asking. The younger doctor had escorted another nurse; the older doctor hadn't bothered to go to the dance at all. Kate had missed the dance too—and had told all this to the old nurse. 'There's no trap so deep as the one you dig yourself,' the nurse had said.

Was she digging a trap for herself with Steve?

Jo had a couple of visitors the next day while Kate was at work, but Kate still wanted to spend the evening with her. She also wanted to see something of Steve, so she phoned him and asked if he'd like to come round for supper. 'You don't mind me staying in with Jo, do you?' she asked.

'Of course I don't mind. I think you're a very special person, wanting to spend so much time with your sister, and I love you for it. See you about nine.'

She stayed by the phone a moment after he'd rung off. He'd said he loved her. Perhaps it had just been a casual, careless way of speaking. But he'd said he loved her. It was something.

Steve arrived with two bunches of flowers. 'One for each of two lovely ladies,' he said. They were different—a great bunch of freesias for Jo and red roses for herself. Kate put the flowers in water while he talked to Jo. Then she slipped back into the living room to join in the conversation.

It was interesting to watch the way Steve dealt with Jo. He didn't bring up the subject of Harry, but neither did he avoid talking about the man when Jo did. He was, of course, Jo's GP, and Kate soon realised that he had skills that she had never much needed. In A and E she needed tact, of course—she dealt with many anxious, incoherent, sometimes newly bereaved people. But usually her dealings were over quickly. There was no time to form attachments, relationships with patients.

Steve was different. He could be dealing with Jo for many years now; he needed to establish a firm relationship that would last if he was to remain her friend as well as her doctor.

Things seemed to be going well when she went to fetch the supper. Jo seemed to be a little more buoyant than before, taking interest in what Steve was saying. Kate was glad he had come. When she returned, he asked, 'I gather you've got some photos of your time in America—walks and so on. D'you think I could see them?'

She was only too happy to fetch them, and Jo seemed quite interested too. Steve was fascinated by the walks she had done. She told him about the summer heat in Death Valley, but how in winter it was a super place to visit. She showed him a picture of her going down the Grand Canyon on the back of a mule. 'They won't keep to the inside of the path,' she told him. 'They like to walk right on the edge. So often you're looking straight down a drop of some seven or eight hundred feet.'

'I'll stick to seaside donkeys,' Jo said.

Steve was obviously absorbed, and Jo took an interest too, so the evening passed quite quickly.

Quite early on Jo said that she felt tired and would like to go to bed, but she hoped Steve wouldn't go; that would make her feel terrible. So Steve sat in the kitchen as Kate helped Jo undress and slide into bed.

'Was she being tactful?' he whispered as Kate re-entered the room.

'Be quiet and come and kiss me,' she ordered. It was their first kiss since Sunday and she was missing him.

There was a call from Jo. 'Kate, come here—and bring Steve with you.'

Steve frowned at Kate, who shrugged and said, 'Let's go and see, then.'

They entered the little room. Jo switched off the radio she had been listening to, put down the book in her hand. 'There you both are. I just want to say that this is my house…' she paused a moment. 'But if you both want I'm very happy for Steve to stay the night. It's obviously your decision; I just want you to know that it's OK by me.'

'Thanks, sis,' Kate mumbled pinkly.

The night before John went back to Las Vegas, as he had suggested, he and Vanessa invited Kate and Steve to dinner. Penny Kirk—who was an ex-nurse herself—had said she'd come over and sit with Jo, so Kate felt quite happy about it.

They dined at the Royal Lancaster again, which John now thought was a wonderful hotel. The manager had showed him original brickwork and woodwork from the sixteenth century, and after that John was sold on the place.

Now that John had accepted that he and Kate were not going to become lovers, she got to like him more and more. And she could now see why Steve thought that Vanessa was an excellent practice manager. Vanessa loved detail. Everything had to be in its place; no little job could be left for another day. And taking over some of the doctors' lesser responsibilities made her feel important.

Altogether it was a pleasant meal, made more pleasant by a gentle sense of anticipation. Steve was going to stay at the house again tonight. He did quite often, in fact. They were lovers, and that was what lovers did.

'So I go back tomorrow morning,' John said expansively. 'I've really enjoyed my vacation, but there's work waiting for me. And in a month or two Vanessa here is going to fly out and stay for a while in Las Vegas.' He put his arm round her shoulders and squeezed. 'It's a different town from Kirkhelen.'

'You poach my practice manager and I'll never forgive you,' Steve said darkly. 'We can't manage without her.'

Vanessa laughed. 'I've absolutely no intention of staying there,' she said. 'Though John tells me that there are lots of opportunities for medical staff.'

Kate smiled to herself. Vanessa would take to life in Las Vegas—not the walking and the travel, but the lively twenty-four-hour social life. She would fit in at once.

John now became serious. 'There is one thing, Kate—this chance of training for the emergency response team. I can probably get them to hang onto the offer for another week or two, but after that you'll have lost it. I'm not pushing you, but the work has to start, and if you don't come for the initial tests and so on the place will have to go to someone else.'

'I'm not leaving my sister quite yet,' Kate said.

'That is your decision, Kate. But I would say that if you're not at the hospital by…three weeks at the latest, the chance will have gone.'

'Do you think Kate should take the offer, Steve?' Vanessa asked.

Of course Steve knew about this job; Kate had mentioned it more than once. Now he said, 'It seems like the kind of thing she has always wanted. She'd be a super emergency response nurse. This sounds like the chance of a lifetime.'

Kate listened to this and wondered.

Next morning there was a telephone message for her in A and E. Would it be convenient for her to come for a sandwich with Andrew Kirk at lunchtime? She phoned his secretary to say yes, and wondered apprehensively if anything was wrong.

When she got to his office her fears grew. There was Andrew Kirk, and Ben Franklin, the orthopaedic surgeon who had treated Jo's leg. Andrew poured her tea, pushed across a sandwich on a paper plate and said, 'I've been interfering again.'

He didn't look too upset by his confession. 'I've been talking to Jo's physiotherapist and this morning I phoned Steve Russell—her GP. We're concerned about her.'

'She's doing well,' Kate protested. 'I make her do all the exercises, and I think that mentally she's improving. A week or two more and she'll be back in your operating theatre, Andrew, there's no need to worry.'

'Physically I've got no worries,' said Andrew. 'She's going to get better. And I think you have been of inestimable importance in seeing to her mental wellbeing. She wouldn't have coped without you. She's relied on you to a massive extent. But it's time that stopped.'

'Time what stopped?' asked Kate, bewildered.

Andrew said, 'Jo is now strong enough to fight for herself. That's what she should be doing—but you are too good to her. We think you should leave your sister—say for a fortnight.'

'Why don't you go back to America?' asked Ben Franklin.

CHAPTER TEN

'IT DOES make sense,' Steve said.

'Not to me, it doesn't. I think it's a terrible idea.'

At first she had been angry at what Andrew Kirk and his friends had suggested and had rejected the idea at once. But he had asked her to think about it, not to make an immediate decision. Since she knew he had Jo's best interests at heart, she had agreed. She had marched out of Andrew's office and phoned Steve at once. She'd needed to speak to him face to face. They'd arranged a quick meeting at five, when she finished her shift, and now they were walking through the hospital grounds.

'It's six weeks now since Harry left her,' Steve said patiently. 'Her broken leg is mending well and she should be out in the world more. You protect her. You wrap her in cotton wool. You're too good to her.'

'She's not well yet,' Kate said. 'She needs more time.'

'I know it's a hard thing to say, but perhaps you need to be cruel to be kind. Ultimately you'll benefit her. The people who have suggested this care for your sister. I do too.'

'But she needs me! I organise the house, I fetch and cook the food, I get her videos and library books. I do everything for her. I...' Then she realised what she had just said. She was doing so much. And Jo wasn't really an invalid any more.

'She needs to be looking after herself. You know she could do more if you'd let her.'

They paced slowly across the lawns. Kate struggled to decide what to do, to reconcile what her good friends were telling her with her own gut instincts.

'You think I should do it. You think I should go well away—Ben Franklin said I should go back to America.'

Steve hesitated, then said, 'I think the idea of going as far as possible is a sound one. You need to be where Jo can't suddenly call on you.'

She was silent for a few more moments, and then said, 'I'm not very happy about it. But I can see the sense in your arguments, so I'll do it.'

'I think you're wise.'

She had taken the decision purely to do what was best for Jo. Now she started to think how it might affect herself. Ever since she had arrived back in Kirkhelen she had been telling people that eventually she would go back to the States. Now she was being almost forced to go she was less happy about the idea. She was enjoying her life. There was much she didn't want to give up. She wanted to stay in Kirkhelen!

'This will upset Margaret Welsh,' she said. 'She's just told me that a permanent job is coming up in A and E in two months, and she very much hopes I'll apply for it.'

'You're getting on better now?'

Kate grinned. 'We spend a lot of time talking about job opportunities in Las Vegas. Yes, we get on well now.' She looked at Steve thoughtfully. 'You've got something in mind, haven't you? I can always tell when you're thinking—you frown a bit.'

He tried to speak casually, but she knew that what he said was important to him. 'It's my summer holidays in a week,' he said. 'I've got twelve days off. I had hoped to spend them with you. So why don't you take me to Las Vegas? I've never been to America; I'd like to see what I'm missing.'

This was something she'd never even dreamed of. 'You want to come to America with me?'

'I want to be with you wherever you are. And I would certainly like to see the desert.'

'All right, we'll arrange it,' she said.

'Kate, that's marvellous!' He quickly checked his watch. 'Now I've got to move. I've got patients to see. I'll call round tonight and we'll decide on what to do next.' Quickly he kissed her, and then he was striding away to the car park.

Kate walked to the nearest bench and sat down. She had some thinking to do.

Life was now moving too fast. For the past few weeks she had concentrated on looking after her sister and enjoying seeing Steve. She hadn't thought at all about the future, the present had been all. Now that was to change. The vague idea that she would in time go back to America was now threateningly real. Did she want to go? Did she want to leave Steve?

She had been so happy with him. There had been other men in her past, but none of them had affected her as Steve did. She knew he didn't want a permanent relationship. They'd agreed that when the time came they would move on. Perhaps be friends instead of lovers. But now that time seemed nearer, she wasn't happy.

And, sitting there in the hospital grounds, she realised she had really meant those words she'd said to him in the hotel. She loved him. No longer did she want to wander the world, she wanted to spend her life with Steve. But he was happy as they were. She thought she had been honest with him—now she realised she had not been honest with herself.

*   *   *

After the decision had been taken, things moved remarkably quickly. Jo was surprisingly agreeable about her leaving. 'That's not a good sign,' Steve said. 'She should fight more for what she wants. She needs to do more for herself, not have things done for her. She's been too ready to let life slide by her. Don't worry, there's a lot of good friends who will keep an eye on her.'

Margaret Welsh was very sorry to be losing her from A and E. 'You are coming back?' she had asked. In fact, very little had been said about that. Kate was leaving her sister for at least a fortnight. After that—who knew what might happen?

Kate was now an expert on getting cheap flights. An hour on the Internet in Steve's office and she had them both tickets from Manchester to Las Vegas. Both tickets were returns, but... She shrugged. She might come back.

She phoned her friend Lucy and asked her to arrange three days' stay in one of the luxurious hotels on the Strip. If she was showing Las Vegas to Steve, then he should see it at its most excessive. And the Strip hotels were certainly that.

'Don't buy any clothes for hot weather,' she told him. 'We'll get them out there. Vegas is a great place for clothes, and everything is cheaper.'

'I'll bring my good boots,' he told her.

They left on a Tuesday, a week later.

It was odd arriving at McCarran International, the Las Vegas airport. Kate wasn't sure how she felt. She remembered leaving not that many weeks before. Then she had been excited at the prospect of her sister's wedding. Now she returned feeling strangely dissatisfied. But she was also so happy to be here with Steve.

They stepped out of the air-conditioned coolness of the terminal building into the blast of the mid-afternoon desert heat. Here, there was none of the pleasant dampness that she could always feel in the air in Britain. The heat was harsh, dry.

She looked at Steve, clad much like herself in loose shirt and chinos. He looked quite at home in the great heat and hadn't suffered much on the long flight. Like most medical people, he could sleep anywhere. 'What d'you think of it so far?' she asked.

His eyes flicked to the dark crest of the mountain range that was so close to the city. 'So far I think it's wonderful,' he said. 'What do we see next?'

They took the ferry bus to the hire car station and picked up their car. Both were insured to drive it, but when she tentatively suggested that she drive first, because she was used to driving on the right and because she knew the town, he happily agreed. She was glad that he didn't have the masculine need to prove that he could drive anywhere.

'We could have been picked up by friends,' she told him, 'and we could have stayed in someone's house. But I want to be independent at first. In fact, I want you to myself.'

'That's fine by me,' he said. 'So long as you're happy.'

Once you knew what you were doing, Las Vegas was an easy town to drive around. She expertly negotiated the back streets and finally drew into the back lot of their hotel. Their car was valet-parked, their booking confirmed and soon they were on the nineteenth floor, exploring their wondrous room.

'Look at the bed,' he said. 'I've never seen one so big. I could wake in the middle of the night and think I'd lost you.'

'That's an emperor size,' she told him. 'And if you think you've lost me, just give a little shout and I'll wriggle over. Now, maybe we should have a shower each and then you can come and be a real tourist.'

They had set off from Manchester in the morning, and now, after a ten-hour flight, their bodies were telling them that it was night-time. But in Las Vegas it was only four o'clock in the afternoon. Kate knew that the best thing to do was not to sleep, but to hang on till later. Then, the next day, they'd be fine.

The bathroom—gleaming with chrome and black marble—was bigger than her bedroom in Kirkhelen, and the water pressure was tremendous. They washed the stickiness of the flight away, changed clothes and went downstairs.

Steve was amazed at the massive ranks of fruit machines, the constant clink of coins. 'Do people spend all day in here?' he asked in disbelief.

'All night as well. This place is open twenty-four hours a day. Come on, we'll walk down the Strip. It's the best free show in America.'

As ever the Strip—Las Vegas Boulevard—was thronged with tourists. It always was. They bought a vast plastic carton of iced cola each. 'This is the desert,' she told him. 'You drink all the time whether you feel thirsty or not.' Then they walked into the hammer of the heat, automatically slowing their usual fast pace to a gentle stroll.

She'd been away a while, had forgotten the frenetic excitement of this city. They looked at the new dancing fountains outside the Bellagio Hotel. They watched two ships re-enact a pirate fight outside Treasure Island. They listened to the screams of the people on the roller-coaster that looped its way in and out of New York, New York. John blinked at two policemen—guns and staffs belted to their sides, but dressed in shorts and on bicycles. 'We'll have to wait a couple of hours,' she told him, 'in fact we'll wait till it gets dark. Then we'll go and see the volcano erupt. It's quite spectacular.'

'Surprise me,' he muttered.

When they were tired of sightseeing she led him a little way off the Strip and they had hamburgers and Margaritas—she knew where the best were to be had. They even gambled a little—but Steve was more interested in watching the other people than he was in the prospect of winning. 'Best people-watching city in the world,' she told him.

Finally, and by now thoroughly tired, they went back to their room. For a moment they left the light off and stared out of the window at the mad line of lights below—Glitter Gulch, it was called. 'Glad you came?' she asked him.

'I'd be glad to be anywhere with you. But, yes, so far I'm enjoying myself.' He peered upwards. 'Look, I can see the lights of two aeroplanes coming in to land at once.'

He seemed fascinated by the view, so she slipped away. A minute later she returned, stood behind him and pulled up his shirt. Then she pressed against him. She had taken off her own clothes, and her breasts pushed against his back. 'Come to bed,' she said.

They made love on the outside of the bed, the light still off and the curtains still undrawn. From outside, coloured lights flashed and illuminated their bodies. It was different and exciting. It was America.

Next day she took him to see her hospital. There was John to call on, Lucy to visit, other old friends to look up. She made dates to see them all later. It was just the same as when she'd left; there was the same casual camaraderie that she liked so much. But something was missing. This wasn't where she worked any more; she didn't feel at home. It took her a while to realise that she was missing the A and E department in Kirkhelen.

'Would you like to work in this hospital?' she asked Steve. 'If you'd taken all the tests and got qualified to work here?'

He looked thoughtful. 'I'm jealous of some of the equipment that's available. Some tests get done here at once that would take three months to come through in England. The staff is certainly well-trained and dedicated. But there's so many different languages! I know America is supposed to be the melting pot, but…' He shook his head. 'How d'you diagnose when you can't speak to the patient?'

'That happens in some London hospitals,' she pointed out.

'I know. After this, I can see why Kirkhelen seems a bit…well, provincial.'

She had never thought of Kirkhelen as provincial; she loved the town. But she knew what he meant.

On Friday the price of their hotel room doubled, so she took him north, a hundred miles across the desert into Utah. They stayed the night in a little motel just outside Zion National Park. It was cooler there, and they spent three days exploring the massive redstone-walled canyon.

'I can see why you love it here,' he said. They had just climbed out of the valley to a place called Observation Point, two thousand feet up a winding track that ran through gullies, along watercourses and skirted the sides of vast cliffs. Now they could look down and see their tiny car, so far below. 'There's nothing quite like this in England.'

For some reason she wanted to defend her native country. 'England has a lot of wonderful walking,' she said.

'I know it has. But coming here makes me realise why you are a wanderer. There's so much to see—and always more over the horizon. Do you think you'll ever settle down? Live an ordinary, boring life?'

She just didn't know what to answer. 'I've no idea,' she said.

On Monday they drove back to Las Vegas and signed in to the hotel again. Steve was amazed at this. 'Do weekend prices always go up?' he asked. 'I know hotel chains in England where prices go down for Saturday and Sunday.'

'Vegas is a weekend playground for most of California. On Fridays people drive in, or more likely fly in. The population can double. They enjoy themselves, win or lose on the slots, and move out on Sunday.'

'I suppose it's a bit like Blackpool,' he said. 'But I've not seen that many coaches.'

On Tuesday morning she was invited to her formal interview at the hospital. It would take most of the morning. She told Steve that she didn't want to think of him hanging round in some waiting room; she would meet him back at the hotel. He said he would do some shopping—there was a mall just up the Strip and he'd buy himself some clothes. When she got back there was a variety of coloured carrier bags on the bed. 'I shopped till I dropped,' he said. 'Did you get it?'

She didn't answer at first. Instead she pulled off the rather formal dress she had worn, and reached for a pair of shorts. Then, 'I was offered a place on the training course,' she said. 'Don't shout congratulations or rush over and kiss me. They've given me a week to decide whether I want it. So now I need some real exercise so I can think about things.'

Very wisely, the only thing he said was, 'I'll get into my walking gear too.'

They drove out to Lake Mead. It was only a twenty-minute drive and Kate directed him down a side road that ran alongside the lake. After they had driven a few miles they parked, just a couple of hundred yards from the shore, and then set off on a long circular walk that she had done before. 'I want to walk, not talk,' she said.

Three hours later they got back to the car. They were hot and the lake looked blue, cool and inviting. There was no one around. 'Another skinny dip?' he asked. 'Like we did in Bramley?' A minute later they were both in the cool embrace of the water.

Afterwards they sat with their backs to a convenient rock and watched the miracle of sunset over the desert. The sky was laced not only with red, but a dozen other colours. They watched, and as it grew dusk she felt she could talk.

'I've been offered the chance to train as an emergency response nurse, and afterwards be part of an emergency response team,' she said. 'The training doesn't start till Christmas. By that time Jo should be definitely well again.'

'I'm sure she will be,' he said.

'It's quite an achievement just to be offered a place. They turn down a hundred applicants for every person they accept. But there is a downside. If you take a place you are expected to work for the team for at least five years. During that time, your life is not your own. I might be sent anywhere in the world.'

'I think you would be an excellent emergency nurse,' he said. 'You have the physical and the mental qualities necessary. And you've always enjoyed wandering—this would be your great chance.'

'What about us?' Her voice was abrupt.

There was a long pause. It was dusk now. She couldn't see his face and had to read his mood through his tone of voice. He seemed casual, friendly. 'Well, I hope you'll send me lots of postcards. But, in general, we decided upon what we were to each other quite a while back. We're friends before we are lovers. We agreed we would part when it was necessary, that we both want to be singletons. We need to lead life as we want it. That's true, isn't it?'

'Yes,' she said flatly, 'that is very true.'

'You're a wonderful lover, Kate, and I'll miss you terribly.'

That was it. He would miss her. There didn't seem anything more to say. 'Time we were driving back,' she said. 'I'll show you a new route into the north of the city.'

By now it was fully dark. They drove through the blackness of the desert, up a long winding road through a valley to a crest. And there below them were stretched the lights of Las Vegas, the entire city revealed like a multi-coloured fairyland.

Usually she found this view had a magic effect. From here it was easy to forget how much of the attraction was tinsel-thin. But this time she took no joy in the view. It was just—a town.

She should have been happy. She had the offer of a

place on the course, Jo would be well by the time she started, Steve was being reasonable, supportive. Why wasn't she happy?

Because she was in love with Steve. She didn't want to go on the course. She wanted to go back to Kirkhelen with him, to have her own boring little house on a hillside, to see her sister regularly every week, not every year. So why didn't she tell him?

No way could she do that. They had negotiated their agreement a long time ago. He didn't want a life tied down to a family. They felt the same; they were alike. Well, they had been alike.

Steve lay on the bed, naked except for a pair of shorts, and watched the reflections of neon lights flashing across the wall. It was nine o'clock at night, the last night before they left Las Vegas. He felt discontented. Tomorrow at noon they would fly back to Manchester.

Kate would be coming with him. For a while he had wondered if she might stay. She now had so much to stay here for. So far she hadn't actually agreed to take up the place on the emergency response course. But that was a formality; she would do it tomorrow morning.

The reason she was returning was that she still had to see to her sister. She had told him no way would she leave Kirkhelen until she was absolutely certain that Jo was well again. She hadn't told him that she was coming back to Kirkhelen to be with him. Why should she? They'd got that sorted out. All they were was friends.

Tonight she had been invited to a hen party with the soon-to-be-married Lucy. She had told Steve that she didn't mind not going, but he had insisted. 'I'll be seeing plenty more of you,' he said. 'You spend the night with your friends. I'll amuse myself on the Strip.'

So he'd done that. He'd walked up and down a bit, bought a few last presents at the Boulevard Mall. Then he'd come back early and made himself a cup of tea with the Assam teabags that Kate had insisted they bring from England. He didn't feel like looking round the town. Not without Kate.

For a while he stared out of the window, contrasting the neon splendour of the Strip below with the dark line of the mountains in the distance. He loved it, of course, but it soon palled. He was missing the damp of home. Earlier he had phoned the surgery, talked to Vanessa and a couple of his partners. Apparently it was raining in Kirkhelen.

For a moment he smiled, remembering being caught with Kate in the storm near Bramley. Then his smile faded. Bramley and the moors there were his world; Las Vegas was hers.

He stood to walk round the room, flicked the television on and off, picked up and threw down a paperback he had started earlier. He even thought of going down into the casino to gamble—but he knew it wouldn't interest him. He wasn't bored; he was dissatisfied. His life wasn't good enough—and he didn't know why.

The phone rang. Who did he know that might phone him here? Perhaps it was Kate. Perhaps the hen night had finished early and... It wasn't Kate. Of all people it was John Bellis.

'Glad I've caught you in,' John said. 'I thought you might be out having a last walk up the Strip. The thing is, I'd like to come round and see you.'

Steve was a little surprised. John had been working very hard, and they had said their goodbyes the day before. 'I could do with some company,' he said, 'but

you know Kate's not here. She's at a ladies only cele-
bration.'

'I know. They'll be partying till the small hours. But
I want to talk to you. If you go down the street at the
side of the hotel, away from the Strip, about four blocks
down there's a small bar called Peter's. It's a quiet
place. Could you meet me there in about an hour?'

Steve was curious. 'I'll be there,' he said.

In Las Vegas there was always somewhere to drink.
Steve put on the uniform chinos and T-shirt and walked
out of the air-conditioned hotel into the warmth of the
street. He still couldn't get used to being so hot, so late.
It was only a five-minute stroll to Peter's, which seemed
to be a more traditional bar than the casino extravagan-
zas that he had become used to.

John was already sitting at a booth. He stood and
waved to Steve to come over. 'They have some fair
Nevada steam beer here, Steve, like to try it?' A waitress came over, brought the beers, little paper serviettes
and a small dish of nuts.

The two sat opposite each other and nothing was said
until they had sipped their drinks. Steve thought that
John looked thoughtful. He wondered if there was a
problem, but couldn't think how he could help.

Eventually, John said, 'Every doctor knows that there
are some things he wants to put right, but he knows
better than to interfere with. That right? You must know
that as a GP?'

'Well, yes,' said Steve doubtfully. 'Every doctor
should remember that he's not God.' He wondered
where this conversation was going.

John went on. 'I'm sticking my neck out here. You
know I fancied Kate no end—I guess I wanted to marry

her. But she didn't feel that way about me, so fair enough; I can take it.' He drank more beer. 'In fact, I have to take it. I think she'd be very good for this course, and an excellent emergency response nurse. But I also think she'd be happier with you.'

Steve blinked. 'What did you say?'

'I said, I think she'd be happier with you.'

There was a silence. Then Steve said, 'I'm a small-town GP. I'm settled in it, I like it, I'm good at it. I can't go wandering round the world. And wandering round the world is what Kate wants to do.'

'You can't be settled and wander,' John agreed. 'Have you asked her to make the choice—between wandering the world and settling with you?'

'I can't do that! I can't put that kind of question to her? It wouldn't be fair!'

'Who's talking about fairness? And why can't you ask her? You love her, don't you? Why not tell her you love her and that you want to be with her always. Then see if she still wants to wander off into the wild blue yonder. Just stop being fair and be healthily selfish. You might find out that she wants what you want—but doesn't know it yet.'

Steve was speechless. He looked from John to the beer in front of him.

'Drink it,' John suggested. 'Give yourself just a tiny touch of Dutch courage. Think the unthinkable.'

Steve did as he was told, then, 'D'you think…?' he started to ask, but said nothing more.

'I'll order another two while you're thinking,' John said. 'And, tell you what, if I'm invited I'll come over to the wedding. See a bit more of Vanessa—I'd like that.'

Steve stood, leaned over the table and gripped John's

hand with a strength that made the man wince. 'I don't know what I'd have done without you,' he said. 'Now I need just one bit of local knowledge and then I'm off. And, John—thank you!'

'It's been a great hen party,' Kate said, 'and I'm already looking forward to the wedding.'

'You're not staying?'

The other girls were going to whoop it up for hours yet, but Kate had had enough. 'Well, it's a long journey back tomorrow, and I haven't packed yet. See you, Lucy, and I bet you'll be really happy. You go back to the party; I'll see myself out.'

It had been a great party, but for some reason Kate found that her heart just wasn't in it. She called for a taxi back to the hotel. It was early yet; Steve should still be awake.

But he wasn't. The light was off in the bedroom and she could hear his heavy breathing. He was a sound sleeper, she knew; she wouldn't disturb him. A pity, really.

She undressed in the bathroom and hung her clothes in the closet. Then she tried to creep quietly into the vast double—quadruple?—bed. She wasn't in the least sleepy but she'd try not to wake him. She'd just lie quietly and think—about things.

As her head touched the pillow and she wriggled to make herself comfortable she felt something hard in the small of her back. Perhaps he'd left a book there. No, it was too small for that, like a box of matches Perhaps it was some kind of male toiletry.

She reached for it and tried to put it on her bedside table. 'Don't put it down,' a voice said. 'Open it.'

'I thought you were asleep. I didn't mean to wake you,' she said. 'I'm so sorry. What did you say?'

'I said open the box. Put the light on and open the box.'

She pushed herself upright and switched on the bed-side light. There was his smiling face, looking up at her. As ever, she was wearing neither nightie nor py-jamas. 'That's something nice to see in a man's bed,' he said, and she pulled the sheet up over her breasts.

'Stop it,' she said. 'I'm curious now.' She picked up the little box.

It was a grey leather presentation box, with the name of a jeweller on top. Inside was a smaller box, this time in red suede, just the size of... Her heart pounded. Suddenly she was so excited. She flicked up the lid. In a setting of white satin, there was a ring. An engage-ment ring. In gold, a heart-shaped ruby, with diamonds round it. She couldn't speak; she couldn't breathe.

Now he was sitting by her. She could feel the warmth of his thigh alongside hers, the touch of his hip and the strength of his arm as he laid it round her shoulders. He took the ring from its bed of velvet and felt for her left hand.

'If I put this on that finger it'll mean we're engaged,' he said. 'Will you marry me, Kate?'

It was a shock but she didn't need any time to think. 'Of course I will,' she said.

They might have missed their flight. They had stayed awake till the small hours, thinking, planning, deciding. Then they had phoned Room Service. A bottle of cham-pagne ordered at four o'clock in the morning was noth-ing out of the ordinary.

'I want to spend my life with you,' he said, 'and this

will be a partnership. If you want to be a wanderer, then I will wander with you.'

She shook her head. 'I've had my wild times. I want to come home now,' she said. 'I want a house in Kirkhelen. I want you to work at the practice, and to start with I want a job in A and E at the Milner. Perhaps once a year we'll fly over here to see old friends. But this part of my life is now finished. Tomorrow I'll tell them that I don't want the place on the emergency response team.'

'Are you sure? This is quite a change for you.'

'Not at all,' she said stoutly. 'For weeks I've been thinking that…that…that friends was all very well, but what I really wanted was a lover. Actually, what I really wanted was a husband. But you seemed so certain that you only wanted a casual relationship…'

'Perhaps to start with. Then I only kept on saying it because I wanted to please you. I wouldn't let myself think about what life would be like without you.'

She shook her head in wonderment. 'And I kept quiet because you seemed so certain you wanted to stay a bachelor. I didn't want to…harass you.'

'We could have missed each other—just because we were too polite.' He shuddered. 'From now on I'm going to be selfish. I'm going to tell you what I want as soon as I want it.'

'Tell me, then,' she said, reaching up for him. 'Who knows? It might be what I want too….'

EPILOGUE

IT WAS raining when they got home—and that made them happier. The plane had flown overnight, but by some miracle it had never quite got dark; there had been sunlight all the way. While the rest of the passengers had tried to sleep they had talked, whispering to each other, planning, arranging, deciding.

'We can't do anything till Jo is fully better,' Kate had said, 'but I want to announce our engagement at once. And we'll have a party in a few months.'

'Whatever you think is best. After all, I'm still her GP. I can't let her health suffer just because I want to get married.'

Kate had giggled. 'What about my health? I think I'll go for that full-time job in A and E. I like the department.'

At the airport they were picked up by Vanessa. She had offered them a lift and the practice partners had said she could have the time off. Kate was just a bit worried at first, but when she told Vanessa that they were engaged, and showed her the ring, Vanessa seemed pleased.

'I'm only surprised you didn't get married over there,' she said.

When they were on the motorway Vanessa handed two envelopes back to Steve. 'Plenty of official mail,' she said, 'and you can make a start on it when you come in tomorrow. But these two were marked "Personal", so I brought them.'

Steve looked at the two letters dubiously. 'Open them,' commanded Kate. 'I can't stand people who don't open letters.'

The first letter was boring—details about investments from the bank. The second letter was handwritten, and Steve pointed to the postmark. 'I think this is from Amy,' he said.

They had sent Amy a couple of postcards, knowing how much she liked to hear from people abroad.

Steve read the letter first, then expressionlessly passed it to Kate. She read it.

I am so glad that I came here and I'm very contented among my friends. I know now I shall never return to my cottage. It is just a memory, but a happy one. I have consulted Dr Stanmore, who assures me I am in my right mind, and Mr Donnington, my solicitor, who does the same. I am very well provided for. I was left a very substantial pension and, unlike some others here, I do not have to sell my house to pay for my keep. So I may dispose of my assets as I wish. I therefore want you to have my cottage. And if you choose to share it with that nice nurse Kate, so much the better…

'Can we accept?' she asked.

He thought for a moment. Then, 'Yes,' he said. 'We can keep it either as a holiday home, or let it and keep it for our own retirement. On the other hand, it would be a great place to bring up children.'

'We haven't decided how many yet,' she said.

'There's a lot we still have to decide. We need to buy a house, we need to furnish it, we need to start planning for our wedding. Mrs Russell-to-be, you don't know how much deciding you're going to have to do.' He looked rather worried. 'Are you sure you're going to be happy with that? No more living out of a blue rucksack? No more wandering round the world when it suits you?'

'Of course I'm going to be happy. I don't want to wander any more. I want to live in Kirkhelen and have holidays in Amy's cottage. And if we have two little girls they can be called Jo and Amy.'

'Two little girls! If we're going to have that many— ought we to start trying for them at once?'

'Well, soon,' she said. 'Very soon.'

MILLS & BOON®

Makes any time special™

Mills & Boon publish 29 new titles every month. Select from...

Modern Romance™   Tender Romance™

Sensual Romance™

Medical Romance™ Historical Romance™

MAT2

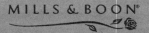

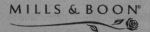

Medical Romance™

THE CONSULTANT'S CONFLICT by Lucy Clark

Book one of the McElroys trilogy

Orthopaedic surgeon Jed McElroy refused to see past Dr Sally Bransford's privileged background and acknowledge her merits. He fought his attraction to her, but as they worked side by side, the prospect of making her a McElroy was becoming irresistible!

THE PREGNANT DOCTOR by Margaret Barker

Highdale Practice

Dr Adam Young had supported GP Patricia Drayton at the birth of her daughter, even though they'd just met! Reunited six months later, attraction flares into passion. Her independence is everything, but the offer of love and a father for Emma seems tantalisingly close...

THE OUTBACK NURSE by Carol Marinelli

In isolated Kirrijong, Sister Olivia Morrell had her wish of getting away from it all, and Dr Jake Clemson suspected that she had come to the outback to get over a broken heart. If she had to learn that not all men were unreliable, could he be the one to teach her?

On sale 6th July 2001

FREE

4 BOOKS
AND A SURPRISE GIFT!

We would like to take this opportunity to thank you for reading this Mills & Boon® book by offering you the chance to take FOUR more specially selected titles from the Medical Romance™ series absolutely FREE! We're also making this offer to introduce you to the benefits of the Reader Service™—

- ★ FREE home delivery
- ★ FREE monthly Newsletter
- ★ FREE gifts and competitions
- ★ Exclusive Reader Service discounts
- ★ Books available before they're in the shops

Accepting these FREE books and gift places you under no obligation to buy; you may cancel at any time, even after receiving your free shipment. Simply complete your details below and return the entire page to the address below. *You don't even need a stamp!*

YES! Please send me 4 free Medical Romance books and a surprise gift. I understand that unless you hear from me, I will receive 6 superb new titles every month for just £2.49 each, postage and packing free. I am under no obligation to purchase any books and may cancel my subscription at any time. The free books and gift will be mine to keep in any case.

MIZEC

Ms/Mrs/Miss/Mr ....Initials ....
BLOCK CAPITALS PLEASE

Surname ....

Address ....

....

....Postcode ....

Send this whole page to:
UK: FREEPOST CN81, Croydon, CR9 3WZ
EIRE: PO Box 4546, Kilcock, County Kildare (stamp required)